The lights were gaining fast. Trying to slow, she moved farther to the right in her own narrow lane, dangerously close to the drop-off into the creek. But the other car—she could make out only the lights and a darkened cab—the other car continued to edge over. Now it was close, and suddenly it rammed directly into her and she was thrown wildly against the door and had to fight the wheel as her small car lurched toward the creek. The other car hit her again, and the steering wheel spun in her grasp and she felt the bone in her arm snap and her car came up on its side then back down and slid through a stomach-sickening 180-degree turn, and she was pointed the wrong way down the road as fenders scraping the asphalt screamed out a trail of angry sparks and two right tires rose off the pavement and the car began to roll and Kathy Sullivan closed her eyes.

BONES

JOHN PAXSON

WORLDWIDE.

TORONTO • NEW YORK • LONDON
AMSTERDAM • PARIS • SYDNEY • HAMBURG
STOCKHOLM • ATHENS • TOKYO • MILAN
MADRID • WARSAW • BUDAPEST • AUCKLAND

BONES

A Worldwide Mystery/April 1999

First published by Thomas Bouregy & Co. Inc.

ISBN 0-373-26306-6

Grateful acknowledgment is made to *Digging Dinosaurs* by John Horner
and James Gorman, copyright © 1988, Workman Publishing, New York,
which provided much information about dinosaurs.

Printed in U.S.A.

To Lucrezia, Shauna and Amanda,
whose intelligence and love have
given me a road worth traveling.

ONE

FAR TO THE SOUTH, maybe fifty miles across the lower mountains, he could clearly make out the summit of Trapper Peak. In the late reflecting blush of the day's failing light, its twin jagged spires seemed to stand as sentinels between the darkening east and the quieting west: a punctuation mark between approaching night and a day that wasn't quite spent. The eastern side of the rigid granite obelisks loomed black and unknowable—inscrutable in a hard and darkened way. The other side seemed almost friendly in a soft outline of copper and orange light reflected from an easy sun almost set.

The young man's lips formed into a half smile as his eyes followed the spires upward. He couldn't make out the exact climbing route from where he sat—it was too far away on the horizon. But he could trace general outlines of the dark chutes up the rock faces and the snowy traverses—the long iced shoulder that rose abruptly toward the western peak. The sinews of his heavy arms tightened reflexively, as though remembering the rocks and the vertical pull, the fatigue and the aching. He had climbed the twin spires enough to know every fold in their hard rock faces, faces deeply carved by ancient glaciers and dotted with silent pools of meltwater.

The man had often sat on this perch and surveyed his world, a world of ice and rock, stunted pine and perpetual snow painted as a postcard on empty sky and dissolving horizon. And what had once been just a good climb had grown into something more. Now it was a place of meditation for him, of discovery—a centering spot high in the mountains off center from the world around. An unnamed ledge on an unknown slope where he could let himself slip into the hard reality of the stone around him, sense his own insignificance in the face of unknowable size and endless time.

The man gazed downward. Nearly 600 feet directly below the lip of the cliff—sixty stories beyond the soles of his shoes—he looked for the small stream that had carved its serpentine path through the mountainside over tens of millions of years. It lay almost hidden in the half light and quiet softness of the approaching night, bounded by slopes of granite scree and tall pines that seemed to rustle one against another to create a low gray hiss on the air. The man strained to hear the faint tumbling of the glacial waters as they scored over the slick rocks and along the branch-strewn banks.

Late May in the high Rockies, and a cold spring seemed to stubbornly linger. The man pulled a blue nylon jacket from his climbing pack and drew it on. He hunched his shoulders, tucking his legs beneath him, centering, closing his eyes. Cold air and, in the slight breeze, a very old silence.

The blow took him without warning, like some giant hammer smashing into his spine, into his existence—an electric bridge of white-hot agony that jumped across his shoulder blades, ignited his spine, and paralyzed his senses. He heard his own ribs snap like dry pine as his back caved in and his body screamed in panic and confusion. His awareness flickered into blackness and then into blinding pain and then into blackness again, his eyes opening and closing spasmodically as contradictory orders leapt across his failing nervous system.

The man pitched violently forward and the mountainside seemed to jump into him, diamond-hard granite gouging into his flesh, crushing his face. He sensed through the chaos that he was rolling forward into space, and he put out his hands and grabbed frantically for the hard rock lip of cliff. It was a hopeless gesture as his fingers closed on the empty air beyond the cliff and he felt his body glide through a clumsy somersault, and he realized abruptly he was falling, realized he was dying. He screamed—a lonely sound that echoed through the hard canyons and came back on itself. He felt his knees bounce from the rock, heard himself scream again, caught a dizzying glimpse of blue sky and black cliff. His body smashed against the cliff wall four times in the seven seconds it took to fall 600 feet. Each contact robbed just a little more consciousness, a little more life, from his form—and lessened the pain. The man was almost dreamily wondering why it was happening to him as his body shattered onto the rocky debris near the small stream below.

JOHN DARNTON

TWO

"YOU SORRY MESS." Tripp said it under his breath and almost to himself, the phrase so common now it was almost a reflex action. And he realized as he came slowly awake that "sorry mess" probably wasn't even a very good description: The words had more to do with people, and his problem was a horse.

Tripp rolled onto his back and gazed up at the broad, long horse's face that had pushed its way through the cabin window over his narrow cot. Tripp sized up the keen eyes above him: The horse had obviously reasoned out that if it could stir awake the sleeping man it could get fed that much earlier. Or possibly, thought Tripp, it didn't have anything to do with food at all. Maybe it was just pure devilment. The cold snout nuzzled down and Tripp jumped from the bed.

"All right, I'm up," he growled, rubbing at his eyes and scratching a hand across the blond stubble going gray. Behind him the horse blew out a snort of anticipation. A large chestnut with a crooked blaze down its long face. Smart eyes that seemed almost to enjoy the view around the small cabin, though what it saw would not impress human eyes: the cotlike bed, a white electric stove and an old refrigerator with coils gone toward rust, a portable typewriter on a brown Formica table, and one battered easy chair wedged amid stacks of paperback

books piled without plan on the floor. A mostly naked angular man standing groggily in the middle of
the room, his hair sticking up at odd angles. The
horse nickered.

"Enough, you equine joke. Move it. Find a lady
horse to play with." Tripp pushed the big head back
out the window and closed the screen, offering up
an exaggerated sigh. But his irritation was mostly
for show. Tripp had come to almost count on the
daily wakeup from the big gelding. It was company,
he realized, and there wasn't much of that around.

Tripp filled a coffeepot and set it to brew. Ran
cold water into a stoppered sink and wet his face.
Began shaving against his reflection in the glass of
the cabin window. Outside, the big brown horse had
returned to a corner of the meadow—a man-made
pasture really, cut from a scrub pine forest—and
joined the two other horses there. Another chestnut
gelding and a brown quarter horse mare with a long
graceful tail—a mix of Arab and something else—
smaller than the other two.

Morning sun was just beginning to find its way
over the pines into the wet grass. Meadowlarks in
the high weeds along the barbed-wire fence dropped
tones of orange and red into the brown morning
silence with their thick calls. As a kid Tripp had
thought the birds were whistling, "Mr. Jacobson's
here." Jacobson was a local tractor dealer and his
visits to the farm were a big deal. Sounded just like
it—to a boy's ears. Mr. Jacobson's here. He'd hear
it in the fields and run up the house to meet the
salesman. Father would give him an odd look when
he said the meadowlarks told him. Tripp couldn't
hear the words now in the larks' morning songs.

Wondered if it was the melody that had changed—
or Ben Tripp.

Dipping a washcloth in the sink, Tripp gingerly
gave himself a quick scrubbing, wincing at the cold
spring water. The cabin's pine and concrete shower
stall was a luxury he used little in summer. Lighting
the furnace to heat water was mostly more effort
than it was worth. Especially if he was carpentering.
Tripp tried to whistle back at the meadowlarks as
he straightened the cot and threw on a T-shirt and
old shorts before moving outside. The tin screen
banged on its hinges.

"Come on, you glue pots, chow's on." Tripp
aimed a garden hose into the carcass of an old
freezer case that served as a watering trough. He'd
have to scrub it out soon, he realized as he played
the stream against stringers of green moss coating
the metal sides. Cold water splashed against his naked legs, and he shivered in the cool mountain air.
The horses pretended to ignore him from across the
meadow.

"Come on, food's on," he yelled, feeding a bur-
lap sack of rolled oats and barley into another
trough. The three gave up the pretense and edged
up, the two big geldings pushing into the feed ahead
of the Arab. Though he still kept saddles and other
tack in the old barn, Tripp didn't ride—hadn't, anyway, since he was a kid. In fact, the horses seemed
almost more of a decoration than a useful tool, a
former city dweller's conceit on an all but derelict
ranch. Tripp supposed that if he had had neighbors,
they would have teased him about owning horses
he never rode. But there were no neighbors around
the mountain meadow. Just Tripp and his horses,

and they'd been hard to refuse—his final payment from a bankrupt builder. He'd made a home for them. Builder's name was Dick Bell. Tripp had named them after the debt: Bella, Bello, and Belli. Tripp hitched a leg over a fence rail and watched them feed.

The little quarter horse, Bella, seemed almost antisocial—as though she knew she was about a half species different from the two big guys and didn't fit in.

Next to her small frame, Bello seemed like a huge horse. Actually, a large horse even for a chestnut. Friendly, Tripp had decided, but not overly bright.

The third, Belli, was far and away Tripp's favorite. The friendly cuss that had poked his nose through the window. A big horse: curious, smart, independent. The horse blew hard, and grain flew in a small circular cloud around the old trough.

Thirty minutes later Tripp pulled his pickup into the wide gravel parking lot of Bowen's Outfitters. Early morning and the store was still locked up tight, a red and black plastic Closed sign hanging crookedly across the door. The wood-frame false front building was in need of a paint job—the bright blue of the Bowen's sign had almost disappeared into the weathered brown facade.

The first Bowen—Ralph—had started the store before the turn of the century to outfit the loggers, trappers, and prospectors moving into the high mountains. Ralph's son had carried on the old man's traditions, now his grandson.

Old-timers would say that grandson Nathan bore a remarkable resemblance to the old man—tall,

black haired, and big boned, slightly stooped as if
he was always trying to put his customers at ease,
to shorten his height, soften some of his body's
rough angularities.

Tripp brought his truck around to the back of the
building and found Nathan draped across an overstuffed red chair on the porch, immersed in the
newspaper.

"Look like a cross between a Grant Wood and
Andy Warhol," Tripp called out to his friend as he
climbed from the truck, his voice feeling unnaturally loud against the quiet morning. "Kind of rustic
camp."

Tripp considered Bowen his closest friend. Probably his only friend. They'd met in the early sev-
enties—Tripp back from Vietnam and aimless,
Bowen taking over his father's store, no war in his
past, no small medals pushed to the back of the
drawer and tucked beneath the underwear. Bowen
had been the one unchanging line in his world as
Tripp got over Vietnam, went through college, married, moved east, divorced, moved west, grew older.
Now the two men in their early forties had coffee
together every Monday morning at the old Bowen
place.

"Weekend?" It was Bowen who spoke up first
when he had poured the coffee.

"Fences, mostly," said Tripp, sipping from a
green mug he'd been assigned by Bowen. One of
the ugliest cups he'd ever seen. A sort of translucent
green carnival glass with a handle in the shape of
a coiled rattlesnake.

"Thought you already rebuilt the fences?" said
Bowen, fixing his friend with a sort of half squint

above a half smile. "You been building those things
for years. Making that a chore, or a career?"

Tripp only sighed. He was thinking maybe he'd
bring his own cup the next time. Go out and buy
something spectacularly ugly.

"Carpentering today?" Bowen asked, smoothing
the paper on his lap and scanning the headlines.
Tripp didn't even bother to glance over at his friend.
Bowen had asked the exact same question almost
every Monday for nearly five years and knew the
answer precisely. Although Tripp liked to tell people he didn't really have a job—or a career, for that
matter—he was good with wood and worked most
of the time as a carpenter. When he wasn't handling
a special order of cabinets or bookshelves in his
shop in the barn, he hired out to local builders and
set down joists, pitched roofs, laid floors. No over-
weening ambition beyond staying busy.

The root of the jibe was that once in a very great
while, Tripp would manage to get himself involved
in what he described as small-time, lame-footed private eyeing: getting paid to snoop around. Purely
amateur stuff, he would tell anyone who thought to
ask. Stray dogs, straying husbands. Bush-league and
small town. He didn't even have a license, hadn't
thought about getting one.

"Other line of work might pick up considerably
if you owned a phone." Bowen offered the observation without looking up from the paper.

"I know that," said Tripp, scanning the far line
of trees at the edge of the river. He'd occasionally
see deer poke from the low willows and make their
way down to the water. "River's quiet this morning." He didn't need to add that he considered

phones intrusive…that there'd been a time in his life when the whole world seemed like one endless telephone call.

Bowen laughed out loud and held up the paper. "Now Lord above, that's a new one." He waved the paper toward Tripp. "Look at this, just look at this. This backwater paper's the best entertainment there is for two bits."

Tripp barely glanced up, only mildly surprised at his friend's animation.

"See," said Bowen, gesturing a thumb toward the masthead of the paper. "Wrong date. They loused it up for real this time. Look at that. Not even the right date this time." He waved the page under Tripp's nose. "I tell ya, Ben old boy, I love this newspaper. It's the dumbest, stupidest, most illiterate paper in the business. Yesterday they ran next week's cartoons and now it's all loused up. Can you imagine how that just wilts the starch out of the yuppies around this state? I mean, the wrong cartoons. And now they can't even get the date right." Bowen let off with a deep-throated, gleeful cackle.

"They had a beaut in Saturday," offered Tripp nonchalantly…and he could tell by the way his friend edged a squint from the side of his eye that Bowen had missed it. Tripp waited. But Bowen wouldn't take the bait. "Saturday, misspelled the president's name," said Tripp. "The president's name. Think that may be a first." Tripp slumped back in his seat with an air of victory.

"Didn't see that one," admitted Bowen, forcing a soft laugh in feigned appreciation of his friend's discovery. He scanned the newsprint hard for more ammunition. The two men had one-upped each other for years over mistakes in the local paper.

"Might also help pay the rent," Bowen said, folding the paper with a snap of his wrists and smoothing the crease.

"What'd help?" asked Tripp vacantly, still lost in beating his friend to the mistake and trying to figure out what the president had to do with his rent. Life on a Monday morning could be more than ordinarily confusing.

"A phone, dipstick. You'd had one yesterday you might not be getting slivers in your hands today. Some woman came by here looking for you. Think maybe she wanted to hire you."

"Me?"

"Alexander Bell. Inventor of the telephone. That's who she asked for."

"What'd she want?" Tripp was fascinated that somebody was looking for him. "Who was she?"

"Didn't tell me either one of those. Told her how to get up to your place. Said thanks and left. She show up?"

"What'd she look like?"

"Looker. Movin' toward late thirties, maybe a little older, but aged well. Dark hair. Nice curves. Beat-up old car. Datsun. Missoula tags. Local, but I don't think I've ever seen her before. Probably university."

"And she didn't say what she wanted?" Tripp hoped the question was casual enough that his friend might not sense how tedious other peoples' wood was becoming. "Was she looking for a carpenter or something else?"

"Didn't ask, didn't say. Smelled pretty good, though, so I suspect it wasn't about wood."

THREE

THE LIGHT was just beginning to die across the canyon by the time Tripp made it home that afternoon. As he leaned from the pickup window for the mail, the battered tin box with its red flag swayed uncertainly on the wooden post. Before him the ranch spread out like a shallow bowl against the pine-covered flanks of the mountains.

The Bells in the field beyond looked up as the truck tires thumped across the narrow steel cattle guard. It was an habitual call to feed, and the horses were gathered at the troughs by the time Tripp parked and climbed down.

"S'pose it's that time again, huh?" Tripp said absently as he began to repeat the morning ritual of dumping out oats and barley. Belli snorted as though in reply. Bella, though, still seemed to hold back.

"Come on, little girl," he said softly. "World's a lonely place if you're all by yourself." Tripp held his hand out to her—but she backed away. "Come on, friendly up, little lady." The mare shied farther and trotted out to the center of the meadow. Tripp picked up a handful of grain and clicked his tongue, but she held her ground, watching.

Tripp washed his hands under the hose and ran a trickle of cold water across his face and down the back of his neck. His face was darkly tanned and lined and, after a day of sawdust and sweat, his blond hair was sculpted into a kind of standing bob. He ran water over that, too, and tried to smooth it down. Didn't work.

Tripp wandered into the part of the barn he'd converted to a wood shop. A large table saw held the center of the room and smaller tools littered the benches on either side. Tripp found a rag and wiped dust from the saw. Pulled a blue tarp back to survey his latest project: a trim six-foot sailboat with plywood sides and a clear Plexiglas bottom. The seams had caulked together nicely, but he still needed to build a rudder and rig some sort of mast. He'd take it to Flathead Lake one day and give it sea trials.

Inside the cabin Tripp whistled as he started dinner: a frozen steak and a factory-made baked potato. Tripp liked to cook but found increasingly it was like heating the shower water—most of the time not worth the effort for just one person. By the time the food was done, Tripp had moved the old Formica table outside under a pine.

Tripp ate slowly, enjoying the approach of darkness. The night seemed to settle—to relax—with the fading light. No breeze, crickets strumming their black and white sounds from the shadows, an owl somewhere off toward the higher mountains offering an irregular brown comma to the night. Deep dusk, and the horses were dark forms against the barn.

Overhead, Jupiter was already shining. Let it get a little darker, Tripp decided, and he'd get out the scope and look for the planet's moons. Guessed it was probably Saturn just edging over the scrub pines. Good clear night to look at the rings. Still chewing, Tripp stood for a better view, but the pinpoint of light remained mostly obscured by the dark trees of the canyon wall to the east. Watching the stars, he walked slowly up the drive toward the cattle guard, away from the obscuring light of the cabin.

Tripp congratulated himself silently as he picked out constellations in the night sky and named a handful of stars. He stopped near the fence line. A single cricket nearby razored its call into the mountain quiet. Tripp made an easy hop to the other side of the ditch. He leaned for a fence post. And missed, lurching in a sprawling, controlled crash and landing nearly on his head in the tall weeds. He sat there for a moment stunned, but astonishment gave way to the silliness of the situation. Tripp started laughing and checked himself for damage. Only his pride, he decided. Struggling to his feet and dusting himself off in the near darkness, he discovered that his right leg was loosely snarled in an old roll of barbed wire. Tripp shook at it, but the tangle got worse. Trying to untie it, he gouged a hole in his thumb. Cursing low under his breath, Tripp arched his tangled leg in a clumsy chorus line kick, but it only sent him stumbling backward in another crash into the weeds. This crash, though, had a spotlight—two spotlights as a car swung across the cattle guard into the drive, its headlights catching him in mid-fall. Tripp hissed out a short curse as he landed on his butt in the ditch, the small cloud of dust rising around him silhouetted in the headlights. The car pulled to a quiet stop and the unseen driver seemed to pause a beat before dousing the damning lights.

The driver's door opened as Tripp scrambled out of the weeds and limped toward the car, dragging a length of wire behind his leg and sucking the gash in his thumb. Trying to summon as much dignity as a man could in the circumstances, Tripp approached with what he hoped might pass for an air of casual elegance. His embarrassment only deepened as he made out the form of a woman. Light-colored blouse, short dark skirt, and high heels. Dark haired. A handsome face—wide dark eyes set above high cheekbones.

"Mr. Tripp?" She was holding out her hand as he approached.

"Howdy," he said, uncertainly, shaking her hand. "Nope, Mr. Tripp was my father"—he forced a laugh—"I'm just Ben. Ben Tripp." He felt dazed by events. And the words sounded astonishingly stupid in his own ears.

"My name's Kathy. Kathy Sullivan," she said. "The man at the sporting goods store" She paused as if trying to remember a name.

"Sorry?" said Tripp, feeling lost. He noticed her car. A brown Datsun. Same car Bowen had mentioned—same woman he'd talked about. "Right, the sporting goods store..." You must mean Bowen's. That's Nate Bowen."

She nodded. "Mr. Bowen told me where to find you. I tried calling, but I guess you don't have a phone?" Tripp winced inwardly, unable to decide whether it was a question or an accusation. "He told me how to get up here, and I came up yesterday, but you didn't seem to be around," she said. Her voice had a deep timbre to it—and a nervous edge.

"Guess I was probably out doing some work," Tripp said. "Sorry I missed you." He thought quickly that the woman had no idea just how sorry he was—sorry that this good-looking woman couldn't show up on a nice Sunday afternoon when he was clean, relaxed, not falling into a ditch like some bum. He decided he'd hire someone to fix the fences.

The woman offered a shallow smile as she looked at the wire still tangled around his leg. "Guess I caught you at a bad time? You okay?"

Tripp managed to peel the wire off. "Surveying the stupid fence line," he said, smiling, "and got all tangled up. You just saw the final act. The opener was something to behold." He steered them toward the lights of the cabin.

The woman laughed good-naturedly. "Must be a lot of work to keep up a ranch like this." She gestured out toward the barn and the darkness beyond. "Is all this yours?"

"Well, yeah, I suppose," said Tripp, wondering if she'd actually seen him falling backward into the weeds. He decided to act like the whole thing had never happened. "It's not much. An old cabin, the barn, and a couple hundred acres of windfall and scrub. Inherited it, actually. From an aunt."

"Nice horses," said the woman, squinting toward the shadows by the barn. "They came up to the car yesterday and were really friendly. One of them tried poking her head into the window." They both laughed.

"That'd be Belli," Tripp said, feeling a touch better. "The big chestnut?"

Kathy Sullivan nodded.

"Yeah, well, he's a nosy cuss," said Tripp. "Never met a window he didn't like." Soft easy laughter. In the light, Kathy Sullivan was a very attractive woman.

"Can I offer you a beer or a cup of coffee or something?" he said, steering them toward the Formica table. He realized too late it still carried the remains of a half-eaten dinner. "Sorry," he said, moving to clear off the debris. "Maid ran out on me."

"Beer?" she said. "That'd be good."

"Comin' up, ma'am." Tripp disappeared into the cabin with the dishes and reappeared with two beers. Kathy Sullivan had settled herself on the single wobbly chair and was looking off again toward the barn. Tripp got another chair and joined her. The light from the cabin cast the table in a soft indirect glow under the boughs of the pine tree.

Tripp judged the woman to be about thirty-eight. Trim, compact, purposeful. Dark brown hair to her shoulders with just a touch of gray beginning to sprinkle through it. Deep eyes—dark green, set wide. A small scar above one eye. High cheekbones and a strong smile. A mouth that could laugh easily. Full lips. Nails manicured red. Long fingers. No ring. She raised the can to her lips.

"Sorry," Tripp blurted out. "I mean, would you like a glass?" He started to get up, but she touched his arm.

"It's just fine," she said. "Look, I'm the one who should be apologizing. Come charging in here, late at night, interrupting your life, and sort of forcing myself into things. Should be me saying sorry. So I'll say it. I'm sorry." Tripp thought to interrupt, but she stopped him with an almost imperceptible movement of her head. "I was talking to the sheriff's people and they gave me your name. Said you sometimes help people investigate things." It seemed as much a question as a statement. She took a sip of beer. "I guess I'm in the market for an investigator." Her dark eyes scanned his face. "Is that what you do?"

Tripp decided there was more wariness in her voice than resolve. "Sometimes," he said. "I mean, I've gotten involved in a few things like that." How to explain to her that it wasn't usually what he did? And that when he did do it, it wasn't all that big a deal? Tripp always felt uncomfortable trying to describe himself. Even when he had a job, a title, and business cards—when he had all the things that identify a life—he was still reluctant to try to describe himself. "I've done that sort of thing a few times before, but it's not been much," he said. He paused before adding: "Or amounted to much, for that matter." Tripp watched her eyes. They were on the beer can, and he thought they looked disappointed. "Maybe I can help, though. I don't know. What is it?"

"They said you were about the only one around," the woman said and took another small drink.

"Suppose that's true," Tripp replied. "Can't make a lot of money in a place this small. Everybody pretty much already knows everyone else's business." He tried a smile and a soft laugh. She smiled back tentatively—but it faded quickly.

"Friend of mine's missing," the woman said, almost hesitantly. But then the words began to flow in a rush. "I think he's been hurt or worse and that's why I came to you, because I'm worried and the sheriff's department says there's nothing they can do. But somebody has to do something and maybe I'm it. I thought maybe you're it, too.'' She seemed startled by her own words. Tripp watched her eyes look off shyly into the darkness. Avoiding his. Nice eyes, eyes he'd like to get to know better.

"Well, I tracked a guy once to Idaho," said Tripp. "He'd been running around, and his wife was getting worried. I mean, that's the sort of thing I've done. And I've had some experience in other lines of work that sort of fit in. So maybe I can help. You've got a friend missing?" Tripp found himself wanting to sound optimistic for a woman who obviously needed his help.

"No one seems interested in it," said the woman. "Police say relatives have to file a missing persons report"—her words were coming again in a rush—"but he doesn't have any relatives, or at least none that care about him. The sheriff said he can't do anything unless there's that kind of report. Or unless there's some sort of strong evidence that laws have been broken. And there's nothing like that. But I know he's in trouble. Or maybe even worse."

"Worse meaning…?"

"Worse meaning worse, I suppose," said Kathy. "I just don't know. But I've got a terrible feeling about it." She seemed to be fighting back tears. "I've talked to a lot of people who know him, but it just hasn't gotten anywhere. You do that kind of work?"

Tripp heard skepticism in her words. Tough to blame her for being skeptical, he thought as he turned the ditch scene over in his mind. "Look," he said, "I do do that. I mean, that's the sort of

thing I do. Not all the time, but maybe I can help."
He realized he was trying to convince himself as
much as he was the woman.

"Okay," she said—but then she hesitated, looking around her as though she'd just realized where
she was. "I mean, well—no. No, I'm sorry," she
stammered. She paused, looked away. "I'm sorry,
but I think this is a mistake. I'm just upset, nerves
on edge." She got up from the table. Smoothed the
front of her skirt.

Tripp felt awkward. And couldn't think of anything to say to make it all better.

"This is really stupid," she said, backing. "I've
made too big a deal out of this and I'm just realizing
it." She headed up the driveway. Tripp followed
her to the car.

"I'm sorry I loused up your evening, Mr. Tripp.
I'm being really very stupid." She held out her
hand and Tripp took it automatically. "Let's forget
about this. No harm, no foul."

"Hey, look," said Tripp as she started the car,
"maybe we could…" But she swung the car in a
tight circle and was headed up the road. "Look,"
he yelled, "if you change your mind, give me a
call."

KATHY SULLIVAN gunned the car down the darkened tunnel of pines, struggling to steer, cry, and
light a cigarette all at the same time. "You stupid
jerk," she hissed at her own reflection in the window of the darkened car, "you lost it this time." A
car loomed up from the darkness ahead and shot
past on the narrow canyon road. She fumbled with
the cigarette lighter and managed to knock glowing

ashes onto her skirt. Tears welled in her eyes and she cursed herself for losing her nerve with Ben Tripp.

"God, you're a twerp," said Kathy Sullivan in the darkness to Kathy Sullivan. "You barge in. Embarrass what's probably a good man. Then insult him." She ran the meeting over in her mind: driving across the cattle guard and seeing him actually flying into the ditch. His stunned expression as her headlights caught him in the weeds. She emitted a half laugh, but the air caught in her throat and she choked back a shuddering sob. The meeting at the table under the pines. His embarrassment over the dirty dishes, his clumsy attempts at putting her at ease. She had liked him very much. And then had lost her nerve. Completely lost her nerve. She felt tears well in her eyes and had to squint them away to see the road. Had lost her nerve and embarrassed both of them in just getting up and running away.

She steered the car through two tight turns and into a long, straight area where the road held a narrow line between low granite cliffs on one side and a rocky stream bed on the other. The rocks flashed past stroboscopically under her headlights, and she willed herself to concentrate on the driving.

Kathy fumbled in her purse for a handkerchief. She glanced up to the mirror to see a pair of headlights emerge from the blackness behind her. The lights were gaining fast, and nervously she hugged the small car farther over toward the looming stream. Bright full beams shot down from the mirror, and she had to turn her head and squint her eyes. The other car pulled out to pass, but something seemed wrong, and Kathy forgot her tears in an avalanche of adrenaline—the other car was moving fast into her lane. Trying to slow, she moved farther to the right in her own narrow lane, dangerously close to the drop-off into the creek. But the other car—she could make out only the lights and a darkened cab—the other car continued to edge over. Now it was close, and suddenly it rammed directly into her and she was thrown wildly against the door and had to fight the wheel as her small car lurched toward the creek. The other car hit her again, and the steering wheel spun in her grasp and she felt the bone in her arm snap and her car came up on its side then back down and slid through a stomach sickening 180-degree turn, and she was pointed the wrong way down the road as fenders scraping the asphalt screamed out a trail of angry sparks and two right tires rose off the pavement and the car began to roll and Kathy Sullivan closed her eyes.

FOUR

TRIPP FOUND HER the next day on the fourth floor of the community hospital. A private room, the sounds of a news program on the television. Tripp walked in softly. Kathy lay on her back under a sheet, a blue and white hospital gown tucked up to her neck. Her hair, splayed out across the pillow, seemed unnaturally dark against the sallow whiteness of her face. A small gauze bandage was plastered across her cheek.

"Guess I showed you too much of a good time last night, huh?" said Tripp gently. The woman's gaze moved down from the television to his eyes and she smiled. Tripp held out a small bouquet of flowers. "Stole these from the funeral parlor next door."

"Howdy," she said, and her voice seemed small. "Come in. They're pretty." She hadn't taken her eyes off him.

Tripp sat down awkwardly on the plastic-covered chair next to the bed, flowers still in his hand. Kathy moved herself up into more of a sitting position and Tripp saw that her left arm was in a cast.

She followed his gaze. "Yeah, quite a sight, isn't it?" She held it up and examined it herself. The plaster began just below the crook of her elbow and extended to her fingers. "Fractured wrist. I must be the luckiest woman west of the Mississippi today." Her good hand touched and lingered on the gauze on her cheek. She seemed to be fighting back tears. "What brings you here, cowboy?"

"Your friend Bowen," he said. "The guy from the store that you talked to about me?"

Kathy nodded.

"He heard it on the radio and came over and told me," said Tripp. "I couldn't believe it."

"Me neither," she said, and used her good hand to switch off the television with the remote control. "It's about the oddest thing I've ever had happen. And I've been in some odd happenings. I'm glad you came." She smiled at him. "You've cleaned up a bit since last night. You look better, and I look a heck of a lot worse."

"You look great," said Tripp, feeling awkward for the nth time and wondering to himself why he had so much trouble with his emotions around this woman, vacillating from juvenile adoration to base embarrassment in the course of a two-sentence conversation. "I mean, you look great, considering what happened. Actually, what did happen?"

"What'd the radio say?"

"That a university professor named Sullivan, a woman, was in the hospital after a serious car wreck up Pattee Canyon."

She thought about it a minute. "Your friend Bowen figured it out from that? He didn't know my name, I don't think."

"Well, he's got a lot of friends at the cop shop." Tripp realized he wasn't quite sure how Bowen had put the two together. "Anyway, radio said you were in serious condition, the car was totaled. Figured I ought to drop by."

"Accuracy of the press, obviously," she said. "A

broken bone and a few cuts and scrapes. Hardly
serious condition. They just kept me overnight for
observation. To see if I was gonna die." She let out
a pinched laugh as hollow as the room. "They're
letting me out today. I don't know about the car,
though."

"What did happen?" Tripp asked again.

"Car wreck, obviously," Kathy said in a voice
thin and tired. "But it was odd. I mean, it was almost as though the other guy was forcing it."

"Other guy?" Tripp was surprised. "Bowen said
the radio called it 'a single-vehicle accident on a
treacherous stretch of road' or something like that.
Didn't mention another car."

"Journalism again." She sighed. "The police
know all about it—or maybe they didn't when they
told the radio station. They just left a little while
ago." Her words came out slowly. Tripp suspected
she might be on some pain medication. "But it
wasn't just me. Another car hit me."

Tripp let out a low whistle. "Bad place to hit
another car."

"I didn't hit another car. It hit me." A glint of
anger in her eyes.

"Gotcha," said Tripp quickly, hoping he hadn't
upset her.

"It was dark," said Kathy, "but you know that—
I'd just left your place. And I saw this other car
coming up behind me and it was no big deal, but
then it seemed to be coming really fast, and when
it started to pass me, it sort of got alongside and
then started coming over. I squeezed farther and
farther right, but there's that drop-off there." Tripp
nodded.

"And I couldn't get any farther over and then it just sort of lunged at me and—bang!—we hit and I went end over end." She closed her eyes. The memory seemed to terrify her and she was quiet for a time. "I came to and they already had me on a stretcher with my neck all taped down to a big board and they were putting me into the ambulance."

"Get a good look at the car?"

"Not even the color," she said. "Just some lights…and then a bang."

Tripp stood and looked out the window. A clear, hot summer day. The mountains shimmered in the distance. Heavy snow still rode the high ridges, but the lower flanks were a deep bluish green.

"So, what do you think?" he asked over his shoulder. "A drunk, maybe?" He hoped that was the answer.

"No," she said, and her tired voice seemed more determined. "I don't think the driver of that car was drunk. I don't think there was anything drunk or accidental about the way that car moved over at me."

Tripp stared at the mountains and considered the possibilities. The driver might have been drunk. He suspected most people in cars on highways after dark were in some state of inebriation. But the woman didn't think so—and she was there. Also, there was the nagging law of coincidence, a law that Tripp had modified to support his own worldview. The law said simply that coincidences don't happen. A woman had almost been killed on the same day she had tried to hire a private investigator to look for a missing friend. Too circular to be coincidence. It broke Tripp's law.

He turned from the window. Gone was the aw-shucks good old boy and with it the discomfort over what had occurred between them. He stood over the bed. "Let's talk about your missing man."

TRIPP EASED HIS TRUCK through the gate of the hurricane fence protecting the police department's impound lot. A scattering of a dozen or so vehicles lined the fence, among them cars, pickups, even an old three-wheeled tractor. A uniformed deputy sorting through the back of a beat-up Volkswagen bus straightened and waved as Tripp pulled to a stop. Tripp knew him vaguely. A cadaverous man with rotten teeth. Friendly but stupid. Moonlighted as a guard at the AmVets club.

"Buyin' a car?" asked the deputy.

"Just pricin'," said Tripp as he walked to the center of the lot where the small brown car of the night before had been dropped by the tow truck. The roof was caved in almost flat on top of the passenger compartment. A whole side, the driver's side, was staved in from front to rear, and the left front fender had been compressed back into the engine block. All four tires were flat. The deputy watched him run his hands over the torn metal.

"Now, I'll give you a real nice price on that baby," he drawled. "Had itself a collision with a mountain and lost." He chuckled at his own joke. "Big Montana mountain just kicked the gizzard outta that little Japanese piece a tin."

Tripp peered inside the driver's compartment. A

tiny gold earring lay on the seat; he slipped it into
his pocket.

"Friend of yours?" asked the deputy.

Tripp shrugged. "What happened?"

The deputy straightened his skeleton under the
baggy uniform. "University woman lost it up Pattee. One of them curves and that little curve behind
the wheel lost it. Bang! Into the rocks. Just dead-
brain lucky it wasn't splash! into Pattee Creek.
She'd a been tuna fish for sure. For sure." Laughing
at his own words.

"Pretty smashed up." Tripp traced his fingers
across a swatch of dried blood on the driver's side
headrest.

"You be smashed up too, you hit that granite up
there, boy." The deputy followed as Tripp moved
around the wreck.

"Lady driving says somebody hit her," said
Tripp.

"Heard that," said the deputy. "Sheriff doubts
it. You show me in those scrapes where he hit her.
I just severely don't think so."

Tripp bent close to inspect the left front fender.
It was so staved in and torn up that he couldn't
make out whether there was foreign paint on the
trim or not.

"That's just purely a mess in there, sir," said the
deputy. "Gonna be tough to say if somebody else
had a hand in that. Real tough."

"What's the word right now on this thing? Single
car?"

"Bet your money on it. Single car. Gonna offi-
cially call this baby a DWF."

Tripp looked over at him.

"DWF, pardner. Driving while female."

Tripp had sometimes laughed at the line before. This time it didn't seem funny.

BACK AT THE STORE, Bowen was waiting on a couple of men in the tackle section when Tripp showed up. After awhile his large friend poured two cups of coffee and joined Tripp at the table near the back. "News, Mr. Headline?"

Tripp winced at the acrid taste of the coffee. "You make this last month? Can't believe people pay you for this."

Bowen gave him a sideways glance. "Some do."

"Went up and saw her," said Tripp. "Not in the worst shape she could be. Broken arm and a cut here and there. She's getting out this afternoon." Tripp didn't add that he'd be picking her up.

"She tell you what happened?"

Tripp shrugged. "Says somebody ran her off the road." Bowen nodded as though it was expected.

"You know something about this?"

"Only cop shop talk," said Bowen. "Word is it looks suspicious, but they haven't found anything solid. Nothing on your girlfriend's car to show another car involved."

"She's not my girlfriend."

Bowen seemed not to hear him. "Deputy I talked to says maybe a drunk swerved over into her trying to get past. Hit-and-run. She say anything like that?"

"Suspects?"

"Whole wide world right now," said Bowen as he rose to tend a customer.

Beyond, the old outfitter's store that Bowen's

grandfather had started still held a lot of the old times. Mounted heads of deer and elk looked down on racks of hemp rope, bridles, saddles, cases of guns and knives that still seemed to draw young boys like flies. The scratched glass counters sat under a ceiling fifteen feet high, where dusty pine beams weathered to the color of tobacco braced wide wooden paddle fans that turned as slowly as the seasons.

"Your girlfriend have any theories?" asked Bowen as he returned.

Tripp realized Kathy Sullivan would always be his girlfriend now in Bowen's mind. "Well, she explained last night why she'd been trying to find me. Wanted someone to look for a missing friend. Guy from the university." Tripp was thinking about the car wreck. "I reluctantly suppose that the two events might somehow be linked."

"Decent supposition," Bowen said, reflecting over another taste of coffee. "What's the story on her friend?"

"Guy's name is Grady, Scott Grady."

"Ah, the good Mr. Grady," offered Bowen.

Tripp shot him a look. "Know 'im?"

"Not in the least," said Bowen with a touch of surprise in his voice. "Should I?"

"Missing," said Tripp. "A graduate student at the university. Young guy. Mid twenties." Tripp found himself reciting parts of the bedside conversation with Kathy almost verbatim. "Worked in the anthropology department, maybe paleontology—the two are connected some way. He and the Sullivan woman are friends. I don't think romantic, but it could be. He'd taken some courses from her. They were friends, like I said. Had lunch together, talked books, stuff like that." Tripp thought about his conversation with Kathy in the hospital. "Get the feeling they were two pretty isolated people who'd somehow connected." Tripp paused, wondering about connecting with Kathy. He pictured her in the half light near the cabin the night before—the deep, almost mysterious eyes, the full lips. Her long fingers on the beer can. "Anyway, about a month ago Grady just wasn't around. Missed a lunch date with Sullivan. She left messages on his answering machine, but nothing. She checked with the anthropology department—or paleontology, whatever—and he hadn't shown up for finals. Called a couple of his professors. They hadn't heard from him. Which was odd as it was right toward the end of the semester and tests were coming up and he should have been around."

"Not all that unusual for a kid to disappear for a while, right?" said Bowen.

"Pointed that out to her," Tripp answered. "But she's pretty insistent that that isn't this guy's style. Responsible is the way she puts it."

"Did the kid travel or anything like that? I mean, what's the past pattern?"

"Yeah, he did," Tripp answered. "Or at least she says he did. He'd go off into the mountains quite a bit. I think he climbs—or climbed." Tripp wondered if the kid might already be a past tense, or if he just felt spooked. "But he always told people where he was headed. Left detailed instructions. You know, the kind of thing that says, 'If I'm not back by Tuesday, look for what's left of me on such-and-such a mountain at the three-thousand foot level.' That sort of thing. Responsible.'' He tasted the coffee.

"Also did fieldwork for his course study," Tripp continued. Kathy hadn't told him exactly what kind of work. "I suppose it was bones or artifacts or something like that. And Sullivan seems to think he was pretty tied up with some project right now. Another reason she thinks his disappearing's a bit off."

Bowen left to ring up a customer. "What's her suspicions?" he asked when he'd sat back down. "She check where the guy lives? What about his car?"

"Think she's completely at a loss," answered Tripp. "Thinks something bad's happened to the kid. Checked the kid's apartment, no luck. Says he rides a motorcycle. Not around."

Tripp pushed his coffee mug aside. "She tried finding him for a while, then went on vacation. Denver, I think. End-of-the-semester break. Like that. Called a few times from there, but he wasn't around. She got back a couple of days ago, and still no kid. Now she's worried. Guess she thought it'd take care of itself. But it hasn't."

"I'll check the boy through the cop shop," said Bowen. "When do you think he vanished?"

"About a month ago. The weekend of May twenty-third. The twenty-third or fourth," said Tripp.

Bowen grinned and crooked a finger as though it were a big fishhook piercing his lip. "Looks like you're gonna be takin' some showers, Mr. P. Mason."

FIVE

KATHY ARRANGED HERSELF on the wooden bench in front of the hospital's main entrance and tried to look presentable. The high heels and skirt of the night before were gone, replaced by hospital loaners: a faded pink gym suit a couple of sizes too big and a pair of men's worn leather slippers. Her cast arm hung in a sling and a small bandage decorated her cheek. She was trying to smooth her tangled hair as Tripp's pickup pulled into the circular drive.

"Lady need a lift?" Tripp beamed as he hurried around to open the door for her. "Lift of spirits? Lift home? Chin lift? Oops, sorry. No chin lift, maybe just a little eye tuck." He laughed—and hoped he wasn't overdoing it. She was at least smiling by the time they pulled away.

"Forgive this old beast of a truck," he said, gesturing around the cab. "Not much for speed, but at least it's not very comfortable." Finally she laughed. And winced as the laugh jarred her arm.

"Sorry about that. No humor from now on. At least 'til you're patched up."

"I'm patched, just not healed yet." She smiled and seemed to relax. "Thanks for schlepping me."

Her place turned out to be a small rented house near the university law school. Yellow and orange flower boxes marked the curtained windows. A large willow had wept its thin branches across one side of the yard. Tripp helped her from the pickup and used her key to unlock the door.

"Whoosh," Kathy said as she gingerly lay back into the cushions of a sofa. "I never in my life expected to be this happy to get home in two pieces."

The room was cluttered but attractive in an academic way: the couch, a chair, a small stereo, two walls covered by shelves crammed with books. A marble-faced fireplace dominated another wall, its mantel strewn with framed photos and a handful of dun-colored rocks. What Tripp decided was an African tribal mask adorned the fourth wall. Below, a set of lethal-looking crossed spears with sharp obsidian tips. A doorway led into the kitchen and, he supposed, the rest of the house. A delicate hand-carved African palaver served as a makeshift coffee table.

"Beer, coffee? What can I get you?" She smiled. "Sounds just like last night—beer, coffee. Good Lord, was that just last night? Seems like a year ago."

"Just stay still and tell me what you want and where to find it," said Tripp.

"Coffee, kitchen, cabinet. Thanks. I'm exhausted."

She'd already nodded off when he returned with the coffee, but her eyes opened as he set the cups down. Blue willow ware. And saucers. Tripp realized he didn't own a saucer.

"Um," she said. "Smells so good. Wow, those pain pills have thrown me."

"Just tell me what you need by way of necessities," Tripp offered, "and I'll make a quick run to the store. Anything I can help you with at school?"

"No," she said and yawned. Tripp imagined taking a nap with the woman. "I'm all set around here. And I'm on summer vacation. Nothing to do for a couple of weeks. Oh, excuse me," and she tried to cover another yawn.

"Look," Tripp said, heading for the door. "You need the rest, and I need to get started trying to get to the bottom of this. Where's Grady live?"

She gave him an address. "But we haven't even talked about fees yet," she said.

"Good coffee's all I ever work for."

TRIPP FOUND Grady's apartment house in a block of once grand homes just on the edge of the university district. A noble house in its better days, the structure had been cut and sawed and reapportioned into a warren of apartments over the years. Metal fire escapes poked out at uncomfortable angles and a clutch of old cars clogged the weeded-over driveway.

Not a wealthy young man, thought Tripp as he hiked up the double-wide stone steps of the front porch. A metal address plate bore the last names of about half a dozen people. He found Grady's next to number five and hit the button. A muffled buzzer sounded somewhere upstairs. After another try, Tripp pushed into the old house, nearly colliding with a young woman coming out in a big hurry. Ratty blond hair and sloppy clothes. But an extraordinarily beautiful face.

"Excuse me," Tripp said, turning after her. The woman kept going. "Yo, stop there a minute.

Stop." The woman turned reluctantly on the steps and gave him a vacant look.

"Looking for Scott Grady up in number five," said Tripp. "Seen him around?"

The girl seemed puzzled by the question.

"Scott Grady?" said Tripp. "Lives in five?"

"Yeah, well," she finally managed to say, "he lives upstairs, I think."

"I know. Have you see him lately, is what I'm asking."

"Not around much," she said. "But he lives upstairs. I think it's five."

Tripp watched her tall, lean body move down the sidewalk before he turned and mounted the stairway. Number five was set off to one side of the house, a middle apartment fashioned out of what had probably been a bedroom. Tripp rapped on the door. No answer. Rapped again. Silence. Tried the doorknob. Locked. He tried number four down the hall. Again no response. Was about to give up when number six at the other end of the narrow hall opened a crack.

"Need something?" said a nasal voice from behind the door.

Tripp talked to the door. "Looking for Scott Grady in number five. Been around?"

The door opened farther, and Tripp could make out the edge of a very thin young man. Mousy hair, glasses, a shirt that hung as though on a wash line.

"Who're you?" asked the shirt.

"Friend of a friend of his. Tripp, Ben Tripp. Trying to find Grady. He been around?"

"Haven't seen him in awhile."

Tripp approached the door and the man started to

close it. "Whoa," said Tripp. "Just trying to get information. You a friend of his?"

"You police?"

"No, not a cop. Just a guy trying to get information. He been around?"

"I only talk to cops," said the voice as the door slammed shut.

"Who collects the rent checks?" Tripp yelled at the closed door.

The voice came out muffled by sturdy wood. "Downstairs. Number two."

Downstairs, number two proved to be an agreeable woman who looked to be in her early eighties. Jessie Humble. She invited Tripp in for tea.

"Afraid I don't have the time, ma'am," said Tripp, standing in the doorway, "though I'd surely love to. I'm checking on a Scott Grady who lives in number five. We've got some important papers for him and he doesn't seem to be around." Tripp suspected Mrs. Humble didn't believe a word of it, but it didn't seem to bother her.

"Haven't seen nor heard from the lad in a month or more," she offered. "He's a nice boy and I do hope he's all right. You're sure you don't want some tea? I'm actually waiting for the painter. This old hall's getting a new coat and then maybe the whole downstairs if the funds can withstand the onslaught. I made tea for the painter. But he's not here yet. Would you like some?"

"Do you know, ma'am, if he's on a trip? I mean, has he paid up his rent and such, like he's expecting to be gone?"

"Well," she said dubiously, "he's only an hour late. And I wouldn't know about his rent."

Tripp laughed softly. "No, ma'am, not the painter. I mean Mr. Grady. Do you think he's on a trip or something like that?"

Mrs. Humble giggled at the mistake. "No sir, and that's strange. That is a very prompt young man. Always pays on time. But he's missed this month's rent. Not like him at all."

Tripp gave her Bowen's phone number and asked her to call if Grady should show up.

It was almost five by the time he found the university's anthropology department: a three-story redbrick building tucked behind the school's sprawling forestry complex. A girl who looked sixteen sat reading a paperback at the reception desk. Otherwise the place was deserted, long halls stretching in both directions.

"Howdy," he said, but the girl barely glanced up from her book. "I'm looking for Scott Grady. Think he's a teaching assistant."

"School's out," she offered in a tone at once condescending and bored. "Everybody's out for the summer."

"I realize that," said Tripp patiently, resisting an urge to order her to her room. "I'm trying to find out if he's been around or if anybody he works with might be available to talk."

"Don't know him," she answered with huge indifference.

"Look," said Tripp, "maybe you have a faculty register or something like that that might tell me at least where he works?"

The girl reluctantly pulled a tattered ring-bound notebook from a drawer. "Name?"

"Grady, Scott Grady." Tripp was beginning to wonder about this whole assignment.

"Brady, Brady...."

He watched her finger course down through the Bs. Tripp interrupted. "Grady, Grady with a G, a Geh."

She found the Gs, found Grady. "TA in physical paleontology. Graduate student."

"Anything else in there that might be helpful?" Tripp asked. The girl only shrugged.

"May I?" he said, taking the book from her hands and scanning through the lists. It showed Scott Grady as a seventh-year student in paleontology, a teaching assistant—a TA. It gave office and residence phone numbers and listed a Howard Donner as his faculty adviser. Kathy Sullivan had told him of speaking with two of Grady's professors, a man named Donner and another named Crossley.

Tripp scanned back into the Ds, found Donner and the number. In the Cs: Crossley, Carl. He found a phone at the end of the hall and managed to make contact with Donner on the fourth ring. Donner was out of breath.

"Sorry," gasped the voice into the phone. "Exercycle's about to kill me. What can I do for you?"

Tripp introduced himself and told him what he knew—or didn't know—about Scott Grady.

"That's a strange one," the Donner voice offered, recovering some of its wind. "Very strange. One of our best people, one of our brightest, just up and leaves. Splitsville. Goners. Can't imagine what possessed him."

"He say where he was going, Mr. Donner?"

"It's Dr. No, nary a word from the boy. Of

course, I come in contact with him very little, you
see. So he'd hardly tell me if he was leaving town.
Nevertheless, it seems a little odd. One day he's
here, next he's gone. I'd hoped to see at least a bit
more of his dissertation by this time. Tell you, the
boy's in serious trouble now.''

"Serious trouble?''

"Academically speaking, of course,'' said Donner quickly. "Dissertationally speaking, if you
will.''

"Anybody he was particularly close to? Who
might know where he went?''

"Boy's quite a loner. But people said he was
friends with some woman on campus. A history
prof? Irish name. Connors? She called me awhile
back. But I really don't know about that. What's
your interest in all this?''

"Just trying to help out a friend of his,'' said
Tripp. "I see in the faculty register that he's a
teaching assistant. Is that a general job? I mean,
does he assist a number of professors?''

"TAs only work for one straw boss at a time,
don't you know,'' said the Donner voice through
the phone. "His overlord is Carl Crossley, paleontologist extraordinaire, if you believe Crossley's
own advertisements. That's who young Scott ap-
prentices for. And that's who you need to talk to.
He and that boy are clones.''

"Look,'' said Tripp into the phone, "I wonder if
we might get together for a brief chat. I...''

Donner interrupted. "Sorry, but it'd have to be
later on. Leaving all but momentarily.''

"Well, when then?''

"Back next weekend,'' said Donner in a genial

tone. "But it's a narrow window of opportunity. In for the weekend then off to London for two weeks. Give me a call. And hey, good luck. Grady's a decent kid, despite Crossley."

Tripp fed another coin into the slot and dialed. This time it was a woman's voice that answered.

"I'm trying to reach a Carl Crossley," said Tripp.

"May I ask who's calling?" said the voice politely.

"Name's Ben Tripp. Trying to locate a young man Mr.—Dr.—Crossley is associated with. Scott Grady?"

The voice seemed to soften. "This is Helen Crossley," said the woman. "I just so adore that young man. And now I'm so worried about him. He's turned up missing, you know."

"That's why I'm calling, ma'am. I'm trying to find him. You expect that your husband would've had any contact with him recently?"

"Oh my, are you with the police?"

"No, just trying to help a friend."

"Oh"—the voice sounded disappointed—"no, I don't think Carly's talked to him—I'm sure he would have told me. We've both just been worried sick about him. But, you see, Carly's not around just now, so I don't know."

"You know when he'll be back?"

"Oh, dear," said the woman. "I don't suppose I'll see Carly for a month or more. You see, he's off on one of his digs, living in some dreadful tent and chasing around after dinosaurs."

"Dinosaurs?"

The woman laughed, nodding. "Dinosaurs.

Sounds strange, doesn't it? Chasing around after dinosaurs. That's what he does, though.''

"Could I maybe call him?" Tripp persisted.

"Oh, I'm afraid not," said Mrs. Crossley. "He checks in with me by phone every week or so, but you can't call in there at all. My, you can barely drive in there."

"Where is there, specifically?"

"I suppose the nearest town is Shelby. That's where I send mail. General delivery to Shelby. But it's somewhere outside of town." Near the Canadian border, Tripp realized, hanging up the phone, about as far north as you can go without leaving the country. One more call by the man who had foresworn telephones. He got Bowen on the fifth ring.

"Anything from the sheriff?" Tripp asked, hoping it all might go away.

"They haven't done a thing," said Bowen.

"Anything on the wreck?"

"*Nada* again, Mr. Holmes. No witnesses, no evidence beyond a few skid marks and maybe some paint chips. She still in the hospital?"

"Took her home," said Tripp. "Still real woozy."

Bowen laughed. "I bet you are with a girlfriend like that."

Tripp ignored the crack. "Nate, do me a favor?"

"You betcha. Baby-sit your new girlfriend?"

"If wishes were horses," said Tripp. "No, I'm leaving town in the morning. Got to find the people who know Grady. Maybe you can take care of the horses for a couple of days?"

"Bring me back a key chain." The line went dead in his ear.

SIX

SHELBY WAS a long day's drive. East out of Missoula for more than a hundred miles to McDonald's Pass on the Continental Divide. A long afternoon driving across the broad lateral foothills that connect the Rockies with the high plains. Tripp brought the dusty truck into Shelby just as the sun was setting.

Three blocks of downtown and quiet on a Wednesday evening. A corner drugstore was open for business but had little. The movie house didn't seem to be operating. A number of buildings stood vacant. Tripp supposed they'd fallen victim to the mini mall he'd passed on the way in.

He could find little evidence on a pleasant June evening that Shelby could be one of the coldest spots in America when January moved into February and winds blew off the Arctic floes up north. And hotter than a blacksmith's shop by August.

Tripp found the local motel and checked in. His inquiries about dinosaur excavations elicited a blank stare from a large and chilly woman behind the desk. He found the Mint Bar and ordered a whiskey.

"Bunch of weirdos out there." The bartender had heard all about the dig and could draw him a detailed map. He leaned over and in a conspiratorial whisper told Tripp it was just one big raunchy party all summer long.

Tripp merely nodded: He'd heard the same kind

of resentment before from others around the state.
Mining and pollution laws were changing the way
people did business—and putting a lot of them out
of work. Academics were easy targets in a complex
issue. He collected his map, paid the bill, and made
his way through the deserted town to the motel.

Bowen seemed to be sitting on the phone when
Tripp called.

"Anything?" asked Tripp.

"Oh, a few odd ends. Somebody apparently
broke into your girlfriend's apartment." Bowen
paused for dramatic affect.

Tripp felt a bolt of alarm shoot through his system. "Nate, is she okay?"

"You betcha," said Bowen almost smugly.
"Happened when she was in the hospital, I think.
She just realized it this afternoon and called me.
Pretty frantic. Think it scared her." Another dra-
matic pause.

Tripp's imagination painted Kathy bloody and
bludgeoned, helpless on her living room floor.
"She's okay, though, huh? You call the police?"

"Reported it," said Bowen. "They were going
to check on it. She found the bedroom window jimmied. I took a look at it. Sort of a ham-fisted job,
seems to me. They broke the molding."

"She's okay, though?"

"Snug as a bug in a rug, Mr. Orkin. Got her
tucked away in my spare bedroom, and I suspect
right this very minute she's dreaming of you."

"Your spare room? At the store?"

"'Bout fifteen feet from where I stand. Seems
happy enough. Maybe give her some chores when

she's up to it. That arm's still hurtin' her a bit. We'll see."

"Anything missing?"

"Nope," said Bowen amiably. "Still has both arms, both legs, the usual."

"Bowen."

"Sorry. No, I got her out of there pretty fast. Didn't stop to do major inventory. Nothing obvious. Where are you?"

"And she's okay?"

"She's okay, Doctor. About the fifth time I told you. Relax. Gonna put her up here awhile for safe-keeping. Doubt anyone would think to look here. Speaking of here, where're you?"

"Shelby," said Tripp. "Sounds like a good plan."

"Cold up there?"

"It's summer, moron. You feed the horses?"

"Nope. Leaving them to die. Especially that walking grease pot Belli. He almost bit off my rear-view mirror. From now on his name's Elmer, pard-ner. As in glue. Adios, amigo."

"Adios," said Tripp. "And take good care of her."

Tripp's mood turned grayer as he lay back against the motel pillow and ran the conversation over in his mind. Many years before, he had begun to do some digging on a politician when one convenient coincidence became two and they were no longer quite so convenient nor so easy to explain. It had taken almost a year. But he'd nailed the man. With the Sullivan break-in added to the car accident, another coincidence had also just become two. He felt around in his pocket and pulled out the small gold earring. Turning it back and forth in the light, he caught his own distorted reflection in the polished metal. "Us against them now," he said aloud to the empty room.

TRIPP STUMBLED onto the site the next morning after thirty-five miles and more than an hour and a half of dusty back roads and ranch lanes winding through a bewildering range of hills and willow-shaded creeks. A compound of tents and tepees and one aluminum trailer seemed to be the headquarters of the excavating operation. A scattering of actual dig sites—Tripp counted five of them—fanned out across a wide area of low rounded hills cut by a small stream. A handful of people worked each site.

Tripp pulled into the compound and made his way to a large open-sided tent where a dozen or so young people were working. Most were in their late teens or early twenties T-shirts and cutoff jeans the dress of the day. Rocks were spread all over a wide table that ran the full length of the big tent. They were being brushed and painted and glued and sorted and tagged, and Tripp realized they weren't rocks but fossilized bones: some as small as thimbles, one pretty good chunk probably a foot and a half long and eight inches thick. Tripp realized it was the same sort of rock he'd noticed on the mantel of Kathy's small fireplace.

At the far end of the table, a young man and a woman were drawing numbers onto the grid of a large poster board. Alongside, what appeared to be a very tall man sat working at a computer.

"Morning," said Tripp and a dozen heads looked up. The tall man uncurled from his chair and threaded through the crowd waving. "Morning," he said. "John Hunt. Welcome to the starship *Enterprise*."

"Ben Tripp. Nice to meet you." They surveyed the room together. "Okay," said Tripp, finally. "Dinosaurs? Right?"

Hunt laughed in a wide, deep voice. "Heaping, creeping, seeping piles of dinosaurs. Big 'saurs, little 'saurs. 'Saurs of all shapes, sizes, colors. You name it, we got it." Grins from the kids around the table. "Any model at all, what's your pleasure?"

"Actually," said Tripp, "I had a more recent model in mind. Trying to find Carl Crossley." Hoots all around the table this time, and a girl at the far end broke into a series of guffaws that sounded remarkably like the braying of a donkey. The infectious laughter spread even to Tripp, though he wasn't quite sure he got the joke.

"Sorry," said the tall Hunt as the laughter subsided. "But Crossley's a tough topic hereand you're not the first to suggest he's a bit of a dinosaur himself." Again grins and soft laughter from around the table. "A friend of his?"

"Never met him."

"Ah." Hunt sighed and his grin spread. "You're in for quite a treat." More titters. Tripp had the sensation he'd stumbled into a Scout jamboree. "But he went into town this morning. Don't expect him back 'til afternoon. Want to wait?"

"Drove up from Missoula to see him," said Tripp. "Don't have much choice."

"Ah, Missoula." It came as a sigh from the man at the poster board.

"Movies," said the girl next to him.

"Beds," said someone else along the table. Then it was like a bidding war among them.

"Hot and cold running food!" said a girl in a blue denim shirt.

"Pizza!" answered a boy in a ponytail across the room.

"Telephones!"

"Television!"

"Dates!"

"Sheets!"

"Dates on sheets!" And the place collapsed in laughter. Hunt led Tripp outside.

"We all love it up here, wouldn't be anywhere else," he said, directing them toward a low hill. "But a couple of months in a tent's a long time. You're not in our business?" It was less a question than a statement.

"Nope," admitted Tripp. "Looking for one of your colleagues, though. Suspect you know Scott Grady?"

Hunt's smile disappeared. "Missing?" Tripp nodded.

"Yeah, figured it was more than just a vacation," said Hunt. "Grady doesn't do vacations." The tall man was leading Tripp around an excavated trench. He seemed to pick his words as carefully as his path, a pensive look on a face that seemed to be carved of right angles. "You police, something like that?"

"Just helping a friend of his who's concerned."

Hunt nodded. "Suppose Crossley's as good a person as any to talk to. He and Grady have a real love-hate relationship, but Crossley knows him probably better than anyone. Grady's Crossley's teaching assistant. But that actually means that Grady is Crossley's slave. It's complex.''

"I've got all the time you can give me," said Tripp. Fifty or so yards below them three students were bent over digging and dusting in the hard clay of a shallow depression cut down through green sod.

"First off," said Hunt, "Crossley's brilliant. Have to hand it to him. Knows his bones. Probably one of the leading paleontologists in the world. A leader in the warm-blooded movement. Big player in the herding concept. Has done some pivotal research on DNA branching and genus typing." If Tripp was lost, Hunt seemed unaware.

"We call him Dino, though," Hunt continued. "Behind his back, of course. Short for Dinosaur. Which is Latin for terrible lizard." Tripp smiled and Hunt chuckled. "Wait 'til you meet him. Judge for yourself."

Hunt explained that Grady acted as the key assistant to Crossley, running his classes and much of his research work.

"What about Grady himself?" asked Tripp. "Smart?"

"As a whip. Known him for a couple of years. He and I are pretty much on the same level of graduate school. In fact, Grady is supposed to be running this dig, not me. But, of course, he didn't show up." The tall Hunt surveyed the compound below.

"I've always thought he'd be one of the greats someday. He was doing leading-edge research as an undergraduate. As an undergraduate. That's almost unheard of. Then, as a graduate, his stuff started getting way out in front of the curve. I mean, this boy is leaving a lot of us in the dust.''

"What sort of stuff?" asked Tripp.

"What do you know about dinosaurs?" countered Hunt.

"Fred Flintstone drove one to work?"

"Let's take a walk," said Hunt, guiding them toward the digs.

"The folks down there in the Morrison," said Hunt, gesturing toward two women and a man squatted down in a trench, "are excavating the fossil remains of a pretty good-sized *Maiasaura*. We call them hadrosaurs. You've probably heard of them as duckbilled dinosaurs?"

Tripp had but didn't know if it was in a textbook or a comic strip.

Hunt spread his arms to indicate the whole area. "This is a veritable cemetery for hadrosaurs, for duckbills," he said. "Crossley was part of the team that discovered that this range of hills—this anticline—hides the remains of ten thousand duckbilled dinosaurs. Crossley got a large part of the credit. Grady did most of the work.''

Tripp whistled in amazement.

"Yeah," said Hunt, "pretty big stuff. Crossley was the number two guy on the team. Number one now chairs his own department at Harvard.''

"Good stuff," said Tripp, squatting near a trench where a shapely woman in a red T-shirt was blowing dust from a protruding notch of bone.

"Great stuff," amended Hunt. "There'd been a lot of speculation, lots of theorizing. But until Willow Hills—that's the name of this area—until the Hills, there'd never been any hard evidence. Now there is. Dinosaurs, at least some species of dinosaur, were herd animals.'' He led Tripp to another part of the complex.

"This is the truly great stuff,'' Hunt said, gesturing to a wide area along the side of a hill. Layers of earth several feet deep had been cut away over a plot of ground as wide and long as a football field. Stakes connected with red tape marked circular patterns in the exposed rock.

"Nesting sites,'' said Hunt. "Where baby duckbills were made—and with them a lot of scientific reputations.''

They knelt next to one of the taped-off areas. Inside, almost two dozen roughly circular knobs about the size of grapefruit protruded from the hard rock.

"Hadrosaur nest, hadrosaur eggs—embryonic duckbills,'' explained Hunt proudly. "A nesting site for baby duckbills.'' Tripp was fascinated.

"Ever since this business started in the mid-1800s,'' said Hunt, "there'd been a kind of common acceptance that dinosaurs were just a kind of very old alligator. I'm oversimplifying, but—''

Tripp interrupted. "Oversimplify at will.''

"Well, that dinosaurs and the ancestors of today's reptiles were pretty closely related. And all reptiles today are cold-blooded, right?''

"Right,'' answered Tripp with more confidence than he felt.

"Right. So dinosaurs were cold-blooded. But weird things kept coming up and science went through some pretty amazing contortions to keep the dinosaurs' blood cold. Along comes Willow

Hills. These nests''—he gestured around him—
"turned the theory on its ear.''

"Can I touch?'' asked Tripp, who had already
snaked his arm under the tape and was petting an
egg. It had the texture of porcelain but looked like
a smooth cylindrical rock sticking out of the hard
ground. Tripp bent close and could actually see the
ancient fracture lines in the shell.

"Once again,'' continued Hunt, "our friend
who's now at Harvard led the research. Crossley
came in a close second and Grady was seen following the parade with a pooper scooper.''

"How'd these nests turn the theory around?''

"Want a graduate or undergraduate lecture?''

"Undergraduate.'' Tripp laughed.

"Basically it's pretty simple stuff,'' said Hunt,
"but it fills volumes. Growth rates of the immature
duckbills in the nests were too fast to be cold-
blooded. So—warm blood. Science turns a corner.''

Tripp whistled. "In other words,'' he said, "the
nests prove that dinosaurs weren't the cold-blooded
lizards we'd always assumed, huh? More like an
ugly Bambi?''

"'Prove' is a tough word,'' said Hunt. "Probably
not prove. That'd be too strong. Sure suggests it,
though. Nothing about this place fits a cold-blooded
animal. Everything screams warm blood. But no,
it's not the rock-solid dead-center proof. First major
evidence, I guess would be the best way to say it.
Crossley's beginning to build a pretty good reputation on these eggs. Grady's getting zip.''

"How good?'' asked Tripp.

"Pretty good,'' said Hunt. "The team leader who
went east on the strength of the herding discovery

is now headed off in another scientific direction. Trying to prove that dinosaurs vocalized. That leaves Crossley as king of the warm-blooded heap.''

"They vocalized?" said Tripp. "You mean they talked?"

Hunt grinned. "Well, I suppose I said that wrong. Not talked. But communicated vocally somehow. There's some bones in the neck that indicate at least that they could articulate sounds.''

"So Crossley's old boss is chasing talking dinosaurs?''

"More or less," answered Hunt. "And Crossley's chasing warm-bloodedness. He's not doing anything that isn't warm blood-related. I suspect he thinks he'll climb to the very top of the heap with the right kind of science.''

"What kind of science is that?"

"Soft tissue," said Hunt.

Tripp looked at him blankly.

"Soft tissue," Hunt said again and pointed around the dig sites. "Everything we get is fossilized bone, right? 'The leg bone's connected to the hipbone'''—the overtall Hunt had begun humming an old song—"'and the hipbone's connected to the backbone.'" He laughed at his own poor singing. "But that's all we get out here. Old bones that have turned to rock. And we draw inferences from how the bones were put together. Show me a fossil lung or a fossil heart and I'll show you proof of warm-bloodedness. But they're just too soft and perishable to hang around long enough to fossilize.''

"You say Crossley got a reputation and Grady got nothing from the work here," said Tripp. "Then it'd be fair to say there's bad blood between the two?''

"No, I don't think so," answered Hunt at length. "I mean not any more than in any professional relationship at school. We all know what the rules are. Work like a demon, apprentice your services to the gods, and someday maybe you'll reach the Pantheon too. I mean...I guess what I'm saying is, Grady knew the rules when he signed on.''

"Know him well?"

"Don't think anyone knows him really well. Keeps himself apart. A lot of people consider him pretty egotistical. My read on the guy is that he's smart and socially kind of graceless. I don't think he ever really learned how to fit in around people, and I think he hides it by being abrupt and a little aloof. Sort of beyond the fray, if you know what I mean.''

Tripp nodded and thought of the little quarter horse Bella.

Back at the central complex, Hunt led Tripp to a fossil-littered table near the main tent and arranged them in a couple of canvas camp chairs. Hunt propped his long legs on the table.

"Okay," said Tripp, "Crossley's a key player in Grady's life. Who else? Others? Men? Women?''

Hunt seemed to reflect on the question, took his time answering. "Donner, Howard Donner. That's Grady's faculty adviser. I think they know each other pretty well.''

Tripp's antennae flashed: Donner had said he barely knew the boy. He'd have to arrange a longer chat with the man. "They spend a lot of time together?''

"Used to," answered Hunt. "Donner's responsible for Grady's dissertation. I don't get the impression that they've worked together on it much, at least not this year. They were doing pretty well last fall, but then it seemed to kind of fade off during the winter. But Grady will ultimately have to have it approved by Donner before he goes before the full staff to take his orals. So they're gonna have to get back together on it."

Hunt seemed to be uneasy over something. It was the first time Tripp had seen it in the friendly giant.

"You said Grady and Donner used to spend time together?" said Tripp, probing. "They don't anymore. Problems?"

"Hard to say." Hunt was quiet for a time. "Look, this is a university. Any university, education's just a by-product of the system. The main thing it produces is rumor."

Tripp sat quietly, waiting for Hunt to continue.

"One rumor has it that Donner's been trying to muscle in on some of Grady's research. Use his dissertation stuff for his own. Can't say if it's true or not true. Barely know the guy had a couple of seminars with him. He just came to the school two years ago. From Nevada, I think." Hunt paused, idly rolling a two-inch-long fossil tooth through his fingers.

"Either Donner or Grady into dope?" asked Tripp.

"Those rumors floated too." He paused again, as if he was collecting thoughts or marshaling arguments. "I honestly don't think so. I mean, if Grady is I've never seen any signs of it." Hunt was silent for a moment, as if he was chewing over words before speaking them. "Honest answer?" he said finally. "I just think Grady outgrew Donner intellectually and professionally. I mean, here's a whiz kid who's ghost authoring some of the best science around and a faculty adviser who's never had a single original idea in his whole career. I just don't think Grady's the type of guy who'd ask a Donner to plan out his life.

"There's also a couple of women on campus," offered Hunt after awhile. "I mean, I think Grady has at least one friend on campus who's a woman. Teaches religions and philosophy."

"I think I've met her," said Tripp without elaboration.

Hunt nodded. "She's new too…arrived a year or so ago. Grady's never talked about her, but I've seen them eating together. I think they're friends. I don't know, maybe they're lovers."

"Lovers?" said Tripp, absently feeling for the earring in his pocket. He hoped they weren't.

Hunt laughed. "I don't know, man. With Grady it could be everything…or nothing at all. As far as his personal life goes, he's a closed book."

"You said a couple of women?"

"Yeah," said Hunt. "Another is—or I guess was—a girl named Corry. Corry Sound. Another graduate student."

"Was?"

"Well, yeah, probably a was. I mean, Corry and Grady were pretty tight last year. Shared some work, hung out together a bit. It got noticed because Grady had always been such a loner."

"But you think that's over."

"I suppose. Or I guess I don't really know. They

worked together last year…actually pretty much all year."

"She around?" asked Tripp. "Sorry, but what's her name again?"

"Corry Sound. Actually it's Corrance. Yeah, somewhere, but I don't exactly know where that is. She spends her summers working for the USGS out in the boonies."

Tripp looked up at him questioningly.

"Sorry," said Hunt. "USGS—United States Geological Survey. Government. Does mostly mapping and things like that. Works for them."

"What do you think's become of him?" Tripp asked finally.

Hunt seemed to study the rocks in front of him and took a long time answering. "Don't know," he said slowly. "Think something bad's happened to him." He paused briefly. "First, Grady just isn't a deserter. It's not in him to leave things undone. And, wow, he's left things undone." Hunt gestured around him. "I'm running this dig in his place. He should have been up here. It's his dig. His and Crossley's. I've got my own ptychodus to fry." He laughed. "Sorry. A Cretaceous fish." Turned serious again.

"Missed semester finals," Hunt said. "He doesn't do that. His behavior was odd going into the finals and all that. But to miss semester finals? I mean, what I'm saying is that this isn't in his known range of behavioral characteristics, as a paleontologist would say."

"Foul play?" Tripp hated the phrase. As though murder or mayhem, though foul, might be some sort of play. Yet there wasn't another phrase that handled it quite so well.

"Maybe," said Hunt. Again his answer was slow, measured. "At first I suspected—I guess we all suspected that he'd fallen off a mountain. Most of us climb a bit, but with Grady it's a religion. I mean, the guy lives to climb. Or climbs to live. When he isn't in his office, he's on some rock face somewhere in the Bitterroots or the Crazies or God knows where. But I don't think that's it."

"Why do you say that?"

Hunt explained what Tripp had heard from Kathy: that Grady had been meticulous about leaving notes on his climbs. Hunt said there had been no note, so probably no climb. "Been thinking about it a lot, but afraid I just don't have a clue," he added. "I just don't have a clue."

SEVEN

BY MID-AFTERNOON Tripp was covered in a fine white dust taking digging lessons at the bottom of a bone-filled trench from the woman in the red T-shirt.

"Looking for Crossley?" said a voice from above. Tripp looked up. The voice belonged to a short man adorned in khaki and epaulets. Thinning hair that looked a little too dark for the face's age was parted low on one side and combed over the top of a sunburned skull.

"I am," said Tripp, scrambling to his feet and emerging from the trench. "Name's Ben Tripp."

"Carl Crossley," he said, shaking hands. "Welcome to the late Jurassic. Is our young lady there"—he gestured to the red T-shirt—"is she taking care of you properly?"

"Most fun I've had in quite awhile," said Tripp. "Never knew what a kick it could be to get down and actually go eyeball to eyeball with a one-hundred-and-twenty-million-year-old ancestor."

Crossley laughed good-naturedly. "Understand you want to talk about Scott Grady?" he said. "Why don't we go to my office."

Crossley's office turned out to be the aluminum trailer, nicely air-conditioned against the afternoon heat. Crossley opened a small refrigerator and popped a couple of beers. Settling into a broken-down armchair, he put his feet on a beaten wooden desk and cradled his hands behind his head. "Young Mr. Grady," said Crossley. "Shoot."

"Spoke to your wife on the phone a couple of days ago," Tripp explained. "She told me how to find you."

"Lovely woman," observed Crossley. "Bedrock of my Bedouin existence. Continue."

"Well, a friend of Grady's asked me privately to look into it. The disappearance?" Tripp formed it as a question.

"Mrs. Crossley and I are very worried about that boy," he said. "Never known him to run off like this."

"You think he ran off then?" Tripp was looking at a strong face: square jawed, framed by a thick neck, creased and heavily tanned, punctuated by a narrow salt-and-pepper mustache. Sharp small blue eyes.

"Don't know what else to think," said Crossley. "To up and vanish in the middle of finals? Think the boy walked on us. Mrs. Crossley and I have had some long, soul searching chats over this. Saddening."

"You say the middle of finals? I thought he turned up missing the weekend before finals. Weekend of the twenty-third. Saturday, May twenty-third."

"Same thing almost. That following Monday morning I had more than three hundred tests to give out and then grade, and no Grady. I must say the boy has burned a bridge, there, let me tell you. Burned a bridge. There I was left trying to deal with all of that and get things ready for the dig up here. Burned a bridge."

Tripp looked around him. "The logistics on something like this must be amazing," he said. "Must be like moving a small army out on field exercises."

"You wouldn't believe half of it if I told you," said Crossley, and Tripp could see in his eyes that he very much wanted to tell not just half but all of it. Tripp nodded his encouragement.

"First," said Crossley, obviously in his element, "first you winnow through the several thousand applications we get from kids all over the world trying to sign into a good dig. And this one's one of the best in the world. Maybe the best. Right here." He tapped the top of his desk for emphasis. "We get the number down to thirty or so, and alternates. Then there's notification, insurance, scholarships, arguments about credits. Just endless. Endless." Crossley sighed the sigh of a tired man. But nothing about him appeared tired to Tripp.

"You do all that or is some of it farmed out?"

"I administer it," said Crossley, emphasis on "administer." "Generally a TA will handle the small stuff. That's a teaching assistant. Or some other graduate students involved in the dig. Then we work on pure logistics. Caterers, camp cooks, water. Water's a real nastiness on these things. I think we've finally solved it here with a tanker once a week. Toilets. Have to have toilets. Generators for computers and lights and equipment." Crossley squirmed around in his chair and pulled a notebook from a rear pocket. He held it up to Tripp. "Know what this is?" he asked. His robust voice seemed pinched, aggrieved. "It's a field book. A scientist's bible. Every event of a lifetime recorded day by day

in here." He made a great show of opening it for
Tripp.

"Know what this page should say, Mr. Tripp?"
He whacked the book against the desk. "Know
what it should say? Should say here, 'Digging in
late Jurassic, major discovery, major discovery, major discovery.' Know what it says instead?" Crossley brought the page close to his eyes. A bit near-
sighted, thought Tripp. "This page says, 'Order
porta-potties,' for crying out loud." He threw the
notebook onto the desk in exaggerated disgust and
took up his pipe, looking across at Tripp with more
dejection in his face than Tripp suspected he really
felt. "Used to be," he said, exhaling a long stream
of thick smoke, "used to be it was you and a pick
and a bone. Load up the old truck. Hit the dusty
back trails. Follow your instincts. But these days
I'm just a glorified bureaucrat." He paused for emphasis.

Tripp let it run.

"Meetings," said Crossley. "You cannot believe
the meetings I must attend. This morning, for instance, our insurance underwriter in Choteau. Over
a broken finger. A broken finger, for crying out
loud. Earlier in the week Great Falls. The board of
regents trotting out pet projects to keep those funds
flowing. What's today?" He looked abruptly at
Tripp.

"Ah, Thursday, I think," Tripp managed to
stammer.

"Thursday...the 25th of June," said Crossley,
consulting a large railroad calendar over his desk.
"This Saturday—and this is just a for instance—
this Saturday I have nine people descending on me

for a four-day visit. Nine people. Four days of dignitaries. Fellow from Yale, another from Denver— both paleontologists of the first stripe, don't get me wrong—a pair of Californians and four Japanese and their interpreter. Their interpreter, no less. And, indeed, I suspect they expect to eat good food and sleep in comfortable beds. Almost a week of wet-nursing."

"Can't say I envy your job," said Tripp. "Was Grady part of all those logistics?"

"Used to be," said Crossley. "First three years up here the boy was really quite involved. Picked up a lot of the load from me, ran a good deal of the logistics and paperwork. Freed me up to do some science. I must say, though, this year the boy has been off his feed somehow. Just didn't seem to have the energy or the drive of years past."

"Any ideas what it was?"

"In this day and age? God knows. Drugs? Sex? Rock and roll? Any combination thereof? Indeed, I don't know." Crossley had taken on a contemplative air, punctuating his sentences with puffs on the pipe. "He just seemed to somehow lose the spark over the last six months. Fell somewhat behind in his class work, seemed almost lazy about taking on new responsibilities. Unlike the old Grady, very unlike him. I guess I shouldn't have been too surprised that he disappeared when the going got really tough."

More puffs. The closed air of the trailer was getting thick. Crossley had taken up a small, crude bow and was fitting an arrow across the string.

"Ever seen one of these?" he said, holding it up for Tripp's inspection. "Paleozoic," said Crossley.

"Or almost, anyway." He pulled the bowstring back and sighted along the arrow toward the window. "Came across a Stone Age Indian camp out near one of the trenches last year. Found this arrowhead." He held the arrow up and admired it close to his eyes. "Quite a beauty, eh? Could be as much as thirty-five thousand years old. Fine piece of work. Predates Clovis, you know?"

Tripp shook his head. "Clovis?"

"Clovis points," said Crossley, smiling. "Early aboriginal American. But I suspect this is substantially older than that. Haven't done the carbon dating yet, but I bet it's from the same population that crossed the Bering land bridge. Had a student build a shaft for it and fashion what may be an authentic reproduction of the bow." He held it up again proudly. "We were where in our discussion?"

"You were saying you weren't too surprised that Grady disappeared."

"Right," said Crossley. "I must say, I see it more and more among our young people. A lack of determination, lack of spine, for want of a better word." He knocked the pipe clean into a hollowed bone on the desk. "Tell me about you, Mr. Tripp? Are you a professional in these matters?"

Tripp laughed. "Not even a good amateur," he said. "But a friend asked, so I thought I'd make a few inquiries. Police aren't interested because there's no evidence of a crime. Thought I'd ask around a bit to see what turned up."

"Who else have you talked to?"

"Well," said Tripp, "quite a few of your students today—John Hunt particularly."

"Good man," Crossley said. "Running this

show in Grady's stead. Dependable, gets it done. Perhaps not as much spark in the plug as Grady—but gets it done. He have anything for you?''

"Just background," said Tripp. "Much the same as you. Talked briefly on the phone with his faculty adviser. Howard Donner?''

"Phew," said Crossley, "strange man. Never thought he was good for that boy. Just not the man to be his adviser.''

"How so?''

"How do I say this delicately?" Crossley paused as though searching for words. "Grady is probably a genius. I mean that. Genius level IQ. But the boy is a loner, a social outcast, a hungry young man in search of a direction in his life. And trust me, Howard Donner is the last man you'd want offering direction to any young man." Crossley picked up the arrow again, absently running the point between his fingers.

"Are they close?''

"Originally, yes," said Crossley. "But I understand there'd been something of a falling-out. In fact, that generally coincides with the onset of Grady's malaise, for want of a better word." Crossley had the arrow on the bowstring again and was sighting absently toward the window.

"You think it had to do with Donner?''

"I can't say that I know. But the coincidence is remarkable. Have you talked yet with the young woman with whom Grady's friendly?''

Tripp pretended to search his memory. "That would be, ah, Sullivan, Kathy Sullivan?''

"Well, yes, I suppose that's her name," said Crossley affably. "Pleasant sort. She, too, apparently is looking into this. She called me just as finals were getting started, and we chatted for a time. Seemed very concerned for the boy. Afraid I couldn't offer much beyond sympathy.''

"Another name I ran into," said Tripp. "Corry Sound?"

Crossley fiddled with the bow. "Of course. Ms. Sound. Not quite as recent. A fellow graduate student. They worked together, it seems to me."

Suddenly the arrow shot from Crossley's lap, caromed off the hard Formica wallboard, and hit Tripp squarely in the thigh.

"Yeeeeah!" shouted Tripp as he leapt from the chair and lunged to the side, pulling the arrow from his leg.

"My God!" said Crossley, scrambling around from behind his desk. "Oh dear Lord! Are you hurt?"

Tripp held the arrow up and looked at the point. A small smudge of blood. He looked down at his thigh. A tiny drop of blood stained a half-inch slit in his blue jeans. "You shot me," he said, disbelief mingling with laughter as he looked at the small wound.

"Good God, man," said Crossley in a near panic. "Nothing like this has ever happened before. Good God, man, it wasn't as though I was aiming at you or anything like that. Here, let me tend to it. Is it bad?"

"Just a nick," said Tripp, who was having trouble believing he'd just been shot with a 35,000-year-old-arrow. He rubbed the hole in his jeans and the skin below tingled. Tripp started chuckling. "Sorry, Professor, but that's one of the strangest things I've ever had happen." He laughed out loud. Crossley stood there squinting uncertainly.

"Sorry," said Tripp finally when he'd gotten his laughter under control. "Just a nick. Nothing to worry about. No harm done. It's just...absurd," and he started laughing again.

Crossley ran his hands through his thinning hair and returned uncertainly to his chair behind the desk.

"You're all right, then?" he said, worrying his mustache with his fingers.

"I'm fine," said Tripp. "Got a whole new war story to tell friends."

Crossley still looked as if he was about to have a nervous breakdown. "I do apologize," he said. "Nothing like that has ever happened before. I do apologize." Crossley self-consciously tucked the bow below his desk.

"Let's go on," said Tripp, rubbing the small hole in his leg. "Corry Sound? Good student?"

"I really can't tell you how sorry I am," said Crossley. "I do apologize. That was very stupid on my part."

"Not much harm done," said Tripp, grinning. "Corry Sound?"

Crossley worked to collect himself. "Okay, Corry," he said. "Yes, Corry. Well...problematic." The professor was still fidgeting in the chair, and Tripp waited for him to settle down.

"How's the Sound woman problematic?"

Crossley's eyes focused back on Tripp and he appeared to come back into the conversation. "You know, Mr. Tripp, we have some of the finest students in the country these days. Good kids, good brains. Really, they're decent sorts. I'd not be the one to ever tell them that, certainly. But they're okay. Corry, though, just hasn't the drive. Maybe she lacks organization. Just a bloody difficult time getting her to focus. Could have graduated that young lady a year ago if she'd gotten her act together. Brainy, she is. Very, very smart. But delay, delay, delay. Almost as though getting it done frightens her. That she'd then have to emerge into the cold world and actually make a living. That sort of thing. Decent sort of young lady...but just not, not focused.''

They were interrupted briefly as a young man came in and handed Crossley a clipboard to sign.

''Well,'' said Tripp, rising from his chair. The stinging in his leg had subsided. ''You're obviously a busy man here, Professor Crossley. Just a couple more things, if I may.''

''Certainly.''

''Mountain climbing,'' said Tripp. ''Seems to be something of an obsession with Grady?''

''Obsession? I think 'compulsion' would be a better word. He's always up in the rocks somewhere, especially recently. You need Grady, he's out climbing. So, yes, compulsion, obsession.''

''I understood he left trip notes? I mean, notes about what he was doing and where?''

''Again, yes,'' said Crossley, rising from behind the desk and moving toward the door. ''Or, let me say I understand that to be true. That was the talk in the office. I seldom bothered with that sort of thing.''

''Recall hearing anything about a note before his disappearance?''

"No, I can't say that the topic was brought to my attention." Crossley puffed on his pipe. "Mr. Tripp, let me be clear. I do not think for a moment our young Grady has met his fate on the face of a cliff. I think he has 'moved on down the road,' as they say. And I think that is a misfortune that will haunt him for the rest of his life."

The two men shook hands and Tripp emerged from the air-conditioned trailer limping slightly from a Stone Age wound.

EIGHT

It took Tripp most of Friday to make it back to Missoula, and when he pulled in the sun was just beginning to sink behind the western mountains. He was tired and disgusted. Three days traveling, he'd decided, hadn't advanced things much beyond start. He called from a gas station for a status report.

"Jason returns," said Bowen, cheerfully. "How goes the quest?"

"No fleece," said Tripp into the phone. "How's Kathy?"

"Helping me close up the store this very minute. Think she's found a second career." Bowen covered the receiver and Tripp listened to a full minute of garbled mumbling. "Sorry," he said as he came back on, "but your girlfriend's a bit confused about the word 'broom.' College degrees ain't what they used to be." He was laughing.

"So everything's okay there?" asked Tripp, feeling left out of things. He caught his own reflection in the glass wall of the phone booth: He needed a shave and a shower. He tried to stand up straighter and checked his profile in the glass. Still looked forty plus. "Everything okay?"

"Fine. She's a bit antsy to decamp. Can't blame her, actually. I'd hate to be marooned in this backwater myself. But she's fine. What progress?"

"Met a couple of people who know Grady," said Tripp, who decided on the spot to omit any mention of bows and arrows. "But I can't say it furthered anything. Opinion's about evenly divided. One side thinks he bought it on a mountain, the other says he took a hike."

"Going to take a lot of work," said Bowen. "Unless he just sort of drops by one day and waves. Then we might be able to figure out he's back."

"Lots of jealousy," said Tripp. "Grady's apparently pretty good at what he does, and his professors seem to be tripping over one another to get at his stuff." Again the receiver was covered and again all Tripp could make out was mumbles.

"Sorry," said Bowen. "Kathy says 'hi' and asks if she can buy you a pretty extraordinary sandwich?"

Tripp could make out the woman's laughter in the background and was tempted. But fatigue was gaining rapidly on temptation.

More fumbling on the phone and he heard her voice.

"Hey, cowboy, how are you?" Kathy sounded bright and happy. Tripp realized he'd missed her.

"Is this the Ms. Sullivan?" Tripp asked. "Captain of commerce?"

She laughed into the phone. "You've no idea," she said lightly. "This is fun. So wholly unlike anything I've ever done. Physical labor is not completely disagreeable, even with this wretched cast on my arm."

"Well, do me a favor?" said Tripp. "Watch your step around that boneheaded man. And whatever you do, don't accept a mug of coffee from him. The experience will scar you for life."

"Whatever might you mean, mister?" Kathy giggled.

"I'd like to take you up on the sandwich offer, but I'm dead," said Tripp, "dead and filthy. Been to the other side of the moon and back in three days."

"I understand," she said, and Tripp found himself disappointed with the speed of her answer. Kathy's voice evened out. "Have you got anything on Scott yet?"

Tripp thought about what he did actually have. When it came right down to it, not enough to fill a recipe card. He explained that it was mostly rumors, office gossip. That one professor—Donner—told him he barely knew the kid. That another—Crossley—said Donner and Grady had been tight.

"I've heard a lot of stuff in a couple of days," said Tripp. "Think we should talk about it." He was picturing faces in his mind: Crossley, Hunt, Donner, Corry Sound. All had an orbit around the planet Grady. And one of those orbits, he suspected, might not be what it seemed. "Free tomorrow?" he asked, hoping hard she'd say yes.

"Let me ask the boss," Kathy said and covered the receiver. There was more mumbling.

"Bowen says you should plan a nice picnic at your ranch," said Kathy. "Says to tell you to pick me up here at ten." The receiver was covered again and Tripp found himself getting slightly irked. He hadn't driven all day just to be put on hold.

She came back on. "Bowen says you're to dust off the saddles and make sure you still have fly rods in working order." More whispers. "And he says if you don't have the right gear you can buy—Mr.

Bowen emphasizes the word 'buy'—you can buy any necessary items here.''

Tripp forced a small laugh and said good-bye, agreeing to pick her up at ten. He spent another quarter. Donner answered on the third ring.

''Ah, the good investigator,'' he said when Tripp had identified himself. ''How goes the hunt? Have you led our wayward boy home by the scruff of the scruffy neck yet?''

''Afraid not, Doctor,'' said Tripp. ''That's why I'm calling. You mentioned you'd be home this weekend. I wondered if we might arrange to chat?''

''Free later tonight,'' said Donner. ''Let's do it.''

Tripp was startled—and more than a little chagrined. He needed to talk to him, but he also wanted after this long day just to go home and go to bed. ''Tonight?''

''Busy the rest of the weekend, I'm afraid.'' Donner's tone was expansive. ''Then out of town Monday for two weeks. So let's seize the moment. What's that trite phrase? Carpe diem? Carpe carp? Seize the fish?'' A short, quick laugh.

Tripp agreed to meet him in two hours and got directions, then headed his pickup for the canyon and home.

Night had come down upon Tripp's high mountain valley like a black blanket as he navigated down the short lane and pulled up next to the cabin. The horses were dark smudges hunched against a far fence. A soft breeze stroked the darkened pines, and in the far distance a coyote's abrupt bark hung like a yellow arrow on the black night.

Tripp was thinking about lighting the furnace for a shower as he fumbled inside the doorway for the light switch. The blow staggered him—a sharp, nasty crack to the back of the head that glazed Tripp's eyes with stars and blackness. He lurched to the side, trying to keep his balance, and swung to meet his unseen attacker, but the blow came again—painful, paralyzing, low on the back of the skull—and he felt his system begin to collapse. Tripp reached for the wall but clutched only air as his mind spun downward into a blackness far deeper than the darkness beyond the thin walls.

His next sensation seemed a long time coming, a sensation of peacefulness. Tripp felt his mind floating somehow, as if it was looking down on a warm and sunny scene of great serenity. A feeling that he was emerging from a long, mindless sleep into a rosy day filled with sunlight and cheer: behind him darkness, before him light and warmth. And under it all was music: a vast quilt of music that seemed to grow out of an intricate fabric of cracks and snaps. The quilt underlay everything around and seemed almost alive as it undulated and changed, its complex melodies endlessly rearranging and emerging as short rainbows of moving light.

Then some inner steering mechanism began to assert itself. The feeling of floating grew heavy and began to fade. And the music began to dissolve into the cracks and snaps that a pitch-laden pine log would emit in a campfire. Tripp's brain forced open his eyes. He was on his back. Above him a cloud illuminated by some orange light. Tripp rose onto his elbows, a dull pain shooting down his neck and across his shoulders. In front of him a fire was licking at dried wooden planks, cracking and spitting as it ate into the aged wood. He rolled to his side and onto his stomach, almost blacking out with the effort. In front of his eyes, some sort of metal object that seemed anchored to some higher place, narrowing as it approached the level of his face. Tripp closed his eyes and rubbed them with his fists. Opening them, he focused again. The metal was covered in sawdust and had a small rubber pad attached to its end. He realized it was the leg of some sort of table. Beyond it now he could make out a larger table and a bright blue plastic sheet that caught and reflected the curling tentacles of fire. His mind brought the images together—his workbench—the tarp over the boat. The metal object that had confused him was the leg to his table saw. He was in his shop. Fire snaking along a wall. A stifling cloud of smoke, his clothes reeking with the smell of whiskey.

With extrahuman effort, Tripp managed to bring his knees under him and heave to his feet, fighting a wave of nausea as he clutched the side of the saw for balance. He turned to see that the fire had spread across part of the shop floor and the lower edges of the wall…and was growing. But even as the smoke thickened, Tripp's mind cleared and he staggered from the old barn to the horse troughs, where he uncoiled the green hose and turned it on full.

Tripp ran back into the barn, directing the spray before him. The fire had more than doubled in size and was feeding strongly from a pile of scrap lumber. He aimed the hose into the heart of the flames and the fire hissed and white choking smoke billowed through the room. Tripp squinted his eyes nearly closed and covered his nose and mouth with his sleeve. He kept the water on the fire, coughing and gagging in the smoke, until it was just steam; and then it was over, the fire was out, and he was staggering outside to dunk his head again and again into the water trough and spit and cough out the soot and the ashes.

Tripp lay there in the dust and the darkness for probably five minutes, calming down, taking stock. His breathing was back under control, though his lungs felt sore from the smoke he'd inhaled. His head ached badly and was tender and slightly swollen where he'd been hit. Tripp suspected it had been a baseball bat or two-by-four. His mind ran over the attack and the fire, playing again and again through the two sharp blows that had dropped him to the floor, the sight of the flame as his eyes had come into focus. A pretty good plan, he decided, for whomever had tried to kill him. Knock him out, drag him to the shed, and douse him in whiskey. Then torch it. Tripp started composing the obituary in his head: "Reclusive rancher succumbs to accidental fire set in drunken stupor." Not bad. With the quilt of music still lapping at the edges of his consciousness, Tripp got up, dusted himself off, and headed for the house to get ready to meet Donner. The table stakes in the Sullivan game had just shot up.

DONNER'S HOUSE was an impressive split-level affair dug into the side of the steep mountain that marked the eastern edge of the city. Though it was dark, Tripp knew the view would stretch off toward Idaho.

The professor was standing in the door silhouetted by an antique porch light as Tripp pulled up.

"Welcome!" said Donner, waving. "I trust you had no trouble finding the place, eh? I've had more than a few faint-hearted give up on these vertiginous heights." No outward sign that the man might have just tried to commit murder: Donner looked cool and composed.

Tripp guessed his host to be in his early fifties. His gray hair was cut tight to his scalp and his body seemed to exude a strong masculine energy. Gray eyes to match his hair. His dress was summer casual—black running shorts and a loose fitting black tank top. Donner's upper torso was powerfully built, and Tripp suspected the man spent a good part of his life on weights and machines. He wondered if it had been those beefy arms that had swung the bat or the board or whatever had tried to kill him just a little more than two hours earlier. Tripp caught himself rubbing the back of his head.

"A libation, perhaps?" said Donner, showing him in. "To celebrate your ascent? House wine tonight's a cabernet." Donner led him up a half flight of stairs toward the living room.

After five years in a cabin, Tripp was impressed. Hardwood floors glowed under indirect lights recessed behind long laminated oak beams arching down from a cathedral ceiling. Windows easily ten feet tall looked out over the lights of the city.

Donner's voice broke Tripp from his reverie. "Nice view, huh?"

Tripp nodded, wincing slightly at the remains of his headache.

"I adore this house for many things," said Donner, "but mostly for its view. You can't see it right now"—Donner was pointing off toward the northwest—"but that's Squaw Peak out there. It's Montana's Mount St. Helens, you know, just waiting to erupt." Donner emitted a low chuckle. "Can you imagine? Living in the shadow of such a vast environmental disaster? Believe me, that volcano will erupt one day. Maybe not today or tomorrow, but one day. And no one seems to care. Even I." He laughed and handed Tripp a glass of dark wine.

"Like San Francisco," said Donner almost theatrically, looking out the tall windows at the lights of the town beyond. Tripp realized it was not a new topic for his host. "Can you imagine the people of San Francisco? Sitting right there in the plexus of the San Andreas Fault? Knowing it's going to kick loose one of these days? And probably destroy them? But not doing anything about it. We're such strange animals."

He turned to Tripp. "Please, Mr. Tripp, take a seat. Do be comfortable. I apologize for the sermon"—he chuckled again—"but it's a pet topic. I'm completely fascinated by the ease with which humans ignore threats to their well-being—it's something of a hobby of mine. And now you're here on a mission that plays toward the same issue. Fascinating." He was grinning broadly.

"Oh, I doubt it's all that fascinating," said Tripp, trying to decide whether to rub his aching neck or attend to the spot on his leg still sore from the encounter with Crossley's antique arrow. He was thinking ruefully about his own ability to overlook threats. "I'm just trying to get some directions on where I should look for Grady." He realized he was very tired, very sore, very worn-out. He wasn't sure he was up to a mental wrestling match with Howard Donner. "You're his faculty adviser?"

"But you see," said Donner—he seemed not to hear the question, or to ignore it, Tripp wasn't sure which—"you see it plays toward some of the same themes, your search. Why do people continue to use tobacco when they know it will almost certainly kill them? Live in the shadow of a volcano? On a fault zone? Why do people drink"—Donner raised his glass in mock toast—"why do they drink when they know it's crippling their body? You see, I believe there's some mechanism in modern man that switches off the survival gene." Donner tasted his wine. "It's a seduction, you know. The edge of death."

Tripp realized that if Donner had been his attacker, it wasn't going to be apparent in this encounter. "Grady may have just taken a vacation," he heard himself say.

"Scott Grady?" It had gotten Donner's attention. "Hardly. That man is not a vacationer. No, I think you'll find at base that there's some suicidal behavior involved. Isn't there with all of us?" He was looking at Tripp oddly, almost challengingly.

"You think the kid's suicidal?" Tripp was mildly surprised. It was the first time he had considered the word in connection with Scott Grady.

"Of course, man," said Donner impatiently. "We all are—to one degree or another. But let's look at Scott." Donner moved to the middle of the wide windows. "Scott Grady. Supremely intelligent, attractive, physical, a veritable Adonis of a young man. But—and this is probably the primary indication of his self-destructive tendencies—he's cut himself off from society. He's made himself friendless. And let me point out, that is a self-generated act. It's hard not to have friends. But Scott managed to shed almost all of them. I posit that in mammalian societal structures, self-exile is either a canny sexual come-on—you know, the unusual being sexually attractive—or it's a means of self-destruction. And I've never believed it's sexual with Scott.''

"So, suicide as a subconscious drive?'' asked Tripp.

Donner nodded.

"What about the women?'' said Tripp. "The Sullivan woman? Corry Sound? They play into this?''

"Impressive,'' said Donner. "You've done some homework. Okay, each as a case. Corry. Corrance, as we call her.''

"You know her well?''

"She's a knowable woman, sir, a knowable woman.'' Donner smiled, and it seemed to Tripp an enigmatic expression, but Tripp was also tired and woozy.

"A splendidly lovely young human,'' said Donner. "I'd say nearly perfect in all senses: physically, emotionally, intellectually. Splendid. And utterly unprepossessing. That's why I say knowable. Open and real. No hidden agenda in the woman. She is what she seems. She—''

Tripp interrupted: "She has—or at least had—some sort of relationship with Grady, I take it?''

Donner tightened his lips and seemed to consider the question at length. "I suppose 'had' is the operative word. They did seem to pair. But I think it was an attraction of minds, not bodies. And perhaps it was an attraction that was somehow spiritually consummated, but I would wager high stakes it was never consummated in the flesh.''

"And Corry's with the survey this summer?"

"Indeed, the USGS has her out in the tulles this summer, slaving for minimum wages."

"Know where she is?"

Donner turned and gestured broadly toward the dark beyond the windows. "Out there, sir. Out there." He seemed to study the night. "Hunched around some small campfire right now, I would suppose. She and her dog." Donner turned to Tripp. "She has a dog, you know."

"I didn't."

"Lovely dog. Blue heeler. Smart." Donner turned back toward the darkness. "Cattle dog, I think."

"You like dogs, I take it?"

Donner turned to him almost vacantly. "Dogs?"

Tripp shrugged, wondering if it was the effects on his brain of the last couple of hours or whether the conversation had come unhinged. "Do you know where she's working this summer? Corry."

"Somewhere in the Rubys, I understand. Up toward the head of Rock Creek."

Tripp made a mental note of it. "Kathy Sullivan, then?" he said. "Same sort of relationship?"

"Casual relationship, at best," answered Donner in a tone that had turned snippish. "Unconnected to where the young man's life runs, to where his passions are. Peripheral, very much beside the point. And I'm given to understand the Sullivan woman attracts the Gradys of this world like stray puppies.'' Donner made a wry face. ''A favorite Montananism in these parts, if I may? Grady's 'cut himself out of the herd.'''

''You saw other signs?''

''In a general sense, yes,'' said Donner. ''Look at his work pattern. I understand that before I joined this faculty—I came here two years ago, by the way—before I arrived this boy was a dervish. Tireless in his pursuit of the degree. And, indeed, I had been witness to much the same behavior in my time with the boy…and then it died.'' Donner seemed to notice the glass of wine in his hand and took a sip. ''Died. Gone. Dried up is maybe a better way to say it.'' Donner moved to the stereo and pushed a button. The room was suffused in a soft Beethoven piano sonata.

''When we first talked,'' said Tripp, ''when we first talked you said something to the effect that you barely knew him.''

''Indeed,'' said Donner. ''I feel like I barely know him.'' Donner lowered the music a touch. ''Grady and I were close initially. As close as one could be with that person, I think. He was a loner. I was new and in search of kindred souls.'' Tripp thought Donner had slightly arched his eyebrows over the comment but couldn't be sure. He realized the wine, the fatigue, the pain, and the Beethoven had combined to form a kind of haze over the events around him.

''I thought we had hit it off pretty well,'' said Donner. ''And in fact we did work well together for more than a year. Got the beginnings of the dissertation started, progressed well. Then just about Christmas—last Christmas—he started distancing himself. My attempts to reach him were increasingly futile. And except for the occasional hallway encounter, our contact with each other ceased. That's why I say to you honestly I do not know Scott Grady at all. Not the Scott Grady of today.''

"Any ideas what caused it?''

"Hunches, speculation. That count?''

Tripp nodded.

"Try the good Dr. Carl Crossley." Donner's lips were tight as he pronounced the name. "The idiot savant of our esteemed department.''

Tripp had come awake. "You two are close, eh?''

"I loathe that man," spat Donner. "For who he is and what he is. An utterly contemptible bantam rooster of a little man.''

"Reasons?''

"You don't have the time, Mr. Tripp. Trust me.''

"But you associate Crossley with the change in Grady?''

Donner seemed to collect himself. Refilled their glasses. Stood again before the tall windows.

"Indeed, I suspect Crossley's hand in the change," he said finally. "Crossley, who has ridden to glory for three years upon Scott's broad back? Indeed, Crossley.''

"Why the hard feelings?''

"I don't like the man," said Donner, simply. "You've met him?''

"Briefly." Tripp didn't add that he'd been shot by him.

"In future meetings take along a snakebite kit." Donner smiled at his own joke.

"That bad, huh?''

"Worse. An adder of a man. Wife's a bit reptil-
ian, too."

"I spoke with her on the phone," said Tripp.

Donner grinned. "Just oozing concern over our
dear young Mr. Grady, I'd bet." He laughed nar-
rowly. "She's as big a fraud as her husband. Think
she's tried to jump Grady's bones for years."

Tripp looked up surprised. "Mrs. Crossley?"

"Jumps anything not of her own decade," said
Donner. "Likes 'em young and pretty. Gets awfully
lonely down here with Dino up chasing 'saurs every
summer."

"Grady ever talk about it? About her?"

"Certainly not to me." Donner laughed. "No,
it's almost like Grady is a walking rump roast and
both the Crossley cannibals are perpetually sharp-
ening their knives and licking their lips." He chuckled at the image.

Tripp remembered the sound Crossley's arrow
made as it bounced off the wall and shot his leg. A
kind of fatalistic thwack. Like a cannibal's spear.

"Each has had their own agenda with that boy,"
offered Donner. "And that brings us back to the
original thought of this unusual evening."

Tripp looked at him blankly.

"Mr. Tripp," Donner seemed almost coquettish.
"The ability to overlook instinct and ignore danger?
Scott Grady has that in spades. I'm sure you've
come across his fetish for mountain climbing. Dangerous, obviously. But even more dangerous is Carl
Crossley. Continuing any sort of relationship with
that man-eater is suicidal, don't you see? That is,
for want of a better phrase, the quintessence of self-
destruction." Donner seemed suddenly tired.

"I need to take a look through Grady's office," said Tripp. "Maybe he did climb, and information about it was misplaced. or maybe there's something else there that might give us some indication of where he went."

"I'll arrange it with the reception desk," said Donner. "Headed off to London Monday, but I'll call the desk."

"London?" Tripp hadn't been there in years. "Must be nice."

Donner barked out a short laugh. "Seminars. We spend more time meeting than teaching. Two weeks of talking." The laugh again.

"If this thing turns serious," said Tripp, "the police might become involved. They'll ask if you can account for your actions around the time he disappeared."

"Name the day."

"Saturday, May twenty-third. He missed a date for lunch that day, had been around the day before."

"I keep quite fastidious notes, I'm afraid—an occupational hazard in my profession. One minute." Donner was gone no more than a minute before returning with a small leather-bound book. "The twenty-third of this month past?" he said, scanning back through the pages. "Easy. From Wednesday through Saturday that week, I think—let's see, that would be from the twentieth to the twenty-third. Yes. Here. I was in Coeur d'Alene. A western regional meeting of the forest service. I'm on their advisory board for paleontological excavation. The Red Lion Inn."

Outside, Tripp wandered over to the professor's red Corvette. "Nice car."

"Small self-indulgence," said Donner, admiring the machine in the half light of the porch lamp. "I gave up four-wheel drives years ago. Like more speed."

Tripp ran his hand over the hood. It was warm. "Been out tonight?"

Donner looked surprised. "Well, actually yes," he said. "A run to the wine shop." Donner's eyes formed a question, but Tripp turned away.

"I do say," offered Donner, "call if you get word of the boy, eh?"

Tripp nodded and waved, maneuvering his pickup through a series of tight turns in the driveway. Under his headlights, Tripp could make out all four fenders of the bright red car. No dents, no scrapes—no signs of a recent collision. But a warm engine. Tripp wondered if the car had been at his ranch that night.

NINE

SATURDAY MORNING warm and clear, and Kathy, in jeans and a sleeveless white cotton top, seemed glad to be out and about after three days at Bowen's. She filled the ride up the canyon to Tripp's ranch with tales of working in the store and the people who came through it. The two chestnuts came trotting up as Tripp pulled the pickup into the lane. The Arab stayed on the other side of the pasture.

"Gotta work on Bella," Tripp said to no one in particular, rubbing absently at the sore spots on the back of his head. There was still a small ache from the night before, but it was manageable. He thought about telling Kathy of the attack and the fire, but he decided to wait for a better time.

"Bella's the little one?" said Kathy. "What's to work on?"

"Wee bit antisocial, I think. She doesn't make friends too easily."

Tripp helped Kathy from the pickup, and the geldings nosed up to her like old friends.

"Here," said Tripp. "A good way to buy affection." Gently unfolding the fingers of her good hand, he placed a sugar cube in Kathy's palm. "Come on," he said. "Let's see about Bella."

They walked across the meadow together, the two horses following them along in single file, bees and flies marking the event with a low brown pasture hum. Kathy said they looked like a parade.

Bella watched them until they were within fifty feet before she started edging away. Kathy gestured Tripp to stop, and the big animals behind almost walked over them before coming to a ponderous halt. The woman extended a sugar cube in her hand and slowly began to approach the Arab, speaking softly, soothingly. The little brown horse held its ground before her, nervously. Finally it shyly reached out and nibbled the sugar cube from her hand. Tripp gave Kathy another and she held it out. The Arab was less hesitant this time. The sugar disappeared quickly, and Kathy began stroking the mare's long neck. Bella nosed at the woman's cast, and then at her face.

"Never seen that before," said Tripp softly.

"She's a nice lady," said Kathy without turning her eyes away from the little horse. "Just needs somebody to care."

The woman fed the horse another sugar cube. The two chestnuts figured things out and moved in for the sugar as well. To Tripp's surprise, Bella held her ground as the two approached. Kathy was feeding sugar to all three now, getting nuzzled and pushed about a bit.

"Better adjourn this meeting," said Tripp. "Break your other arm and I'll die from the lawyer bills."

All three horses followed them back toward the cabin.

Kathy's cheeks were red, almost blushing. "I enjoyed that," she said. "That's a nice little horse."

"Think she enjoyed it too," said Tripp. "Never seen her that approachable." Tripp decided not to

add that he'd be pretty friendly too if this woman
fed him sugar right out of her hand.

Kathy was beaming with enjoyment. "Used to
ride quite a bit when I was a kid in Seattle—around
horses a lot. It means so much when you can make
contact like that. That's a nice little horse."

With a picnic box from Bowen loaded in the back
of the pickup, Tripp and Kathy set off for the mountains. Tall pines crowded up to the edge of the road
on either side.

"Like a tunnel," said Kathy, watching the scenery go by. "Had that feeling when I was up here
before. That you're driving through a green tunnel."

At the paved road where a right turn would take
them toward town, Tripp turned left, heading up the
canyon. Kathy watched the waters of Pattee Creek
rushing past them.

"Guess I'm gonna have to get a new car."

"Totaled?"

"Absolutely."

Out of the corner of his eye, Tripp saw a slight
shudder pass through the woman. She remained silent as Tripp navigated several miles up the canyon
road and then turned off on a narrow dirt track. The
pickup tires thumped as they crossed an old wood
plank bridge over the creek.

Tripp maneuvered the truck off the track and onto
a narrow lane that was no more than an overgrown
path through the pines and granite boulders. He
shifted into sub low and the pickup rocked and
bucked as it pushed through a washout. Kathy was
holding her casted arm.

"Sorry," said Tripp. "Haven't been up here in a

couple of years. Didn't know this road's so totally shot.'' He concentrated on driving.

"This is a road?" said Kathy good-naturedly. "More like somebody's bad dream of a road."

"Old mining road," he said. "Imagine a mule pulling an ore cart along this thing? Those old folks worked for a living."

"What kind of mine?"

"Gold," answered Tripp. "Gold and a bit of silver and lead. Mostly gold. Took millions out of these hills at the turn of the century. At thirty-five dollars an ounce. Some heavy lifting."

They came to a high meadow formed in the V of a small valley. Tripp pushed the truck along a barely discernible track that wandered through tall prairie grass and across a shallow stream. A stand of old sheds peeked out from under the pines on the far side like a patch of mushrooms in a tall forest.

"Mining camp," said Tripp.

"Deserted?"

"For almost a century. Used to come up here as a kid and poke through the sheds. Found great stuff. Old bottles and horseshoes and hammers, things like that. Bits and pieces of magazines and calendars, too. Some as late as the thirties."

They parked in the shade of a stand of pines. Tripp hoisted the picnic box to his shoulder and led Kathy up the slope toward the forest beyond. After awhile the ground leveled off and a series of trenches and rock walls poked from beneath the trees. Tripp climbed onto a shallow rock wall. Kathy joined him.

"Old mine—placer," said Tripp, gesturing around him with both arms.

"Where's the tunnel?"

"No tunnel," said Tripp. "Placer."

Kathy nodded, but it was obvious he'd lapsed into a language she didn't speak.

"Sorry," said Tripp. "Two kinds of gold mining—hard rock and placer. Hard rock's the tunnel kind, mostly. Figure out what kind of rock the gold is in and tunnel in and dynamite it out. The gold's in the hard rock. Hard-rock mining." He kicked at the crude wall under their feet. "This is placer. Don't even know where the word comes from. But the gold here is like tiny grains of sand that have been washed down streams and lodged in the rocks and gravel. They pan the gold out of the gravel."

"So there's gold under us right now?" asked Kathy. She seemed delighted.

"Plenty," said Tripp. "They only stopped mining here because the gold was getting too deep and it was costing more to get out than it was worth."

"Placer," said Kathy and she seemed to be turning the word over in her mouth.

"Placer operation," said Tripp. "Bring in water from way up the mountain and wash the gold out of the rocks." He suspected he was probably talking too much, but he enjoyed explaining what had been explained to him thirty-five years before by a patient father. Though his father was now only a dim memory, Tripp could clearly recall the day, the weather, even the exact place where the two had first sat and talked about gold. It was the same spot.

They were quiet for a time. Around them only the distant chatter of a squirrel broke the dry mountain silence. On the air, the soft aroma of summer pine and sandy earth.

"My father and I used to come up here all the time," Tripp said, "even in the winter. Think my dad had a real gold bug. We'd come up and scoop away the snow and get buckets of gravel. Take them down to the stream down there, where we'd have to chip away ice and then pan it out in that freezing water. Man, it was cold. I still remember the cold."

"Get any gold?"

"One or two little specks—and my dad would be as happy as if he'd found the mother lode. Probably a nickel's worth. No more than a nickel."

"Can we come up here and do that sometime?" asked Kathy. "I'd like to do that...with you."

"I'd like to do that, too," Tripp said, and smiled.

The two explored the old trenches and walls for a while and then picked a trail up the hillside through sparse pines and light brush. At the top a rounded knoll dotted with gnarly green clumps of bear grass looked out over the valley and to the mountains beyond. Nearby the waters of a small spring lapped through soft moss and pooled at the lip of a fallen log. Behind them an impenetrable green wall of tall pine pushed up the mountainside.

"Hope Bowen approves." Tripp laughed as he set down the box. "Tripp's secret garden." He gestured around him. "Been one of my favorite spots since I was old enough to say favorite."

Kathy looked around her, turning full circle. A strand of hair had fallen across her face. "It's beautiful, Ben. Ben Tripp's secret garden." She said the words softly, almost as if she was tasting them.

Tripp smiled and began spreading out the contents of the box. "Buffalo burgers," he said. "Rancid cheese. Good, Bowen. Ah, let's see. Two wormy apples. Bag of stale chips. And, of course, Bowen's special reserve," said Tripp, holding up a wine bottle. "June."

They sat back on the grass and sipped the wine. Off on the western horizon, clouds had begun to form around the distant peaks of the Bitterroots.

"Weather coming in," said Tripp.

"Nice place to be from," said Kathy, watching the sky.

"So's Seattle."

"Yeah," said Kathy. "But it's cloudy more than it's sunny. And I didn't spend much time there. Army brat...and we moved around a lot." She picked at a clump of the bear grass. "You move around as a kid?"

Tripp chuckled. "Hardly," he said. "Same country school for eight years. Then I went into town to the big school for high school." A soft laugh. "A hundred kids."

"So you've got roots?" She said it almost longingly.

"S'pose you could say that. But the war and everything. People just sort of went off their own way. Didn't stay close, really."

"You and Bowen go to school together?"

"No. Different schools, different towns. State's a big place. We sort of hooked up after I got back from the war."

"What did you do there?" Kathy asked. Her voice was quiet and her eyes were on the mountains. "You fight?"

"Just survived." Tripp laughed self-consciously

and busied himself unwrapping sandwiches. How to tell a person what he'd seen, what he'd done? How to describe a reality that was beyond description? And it was a long time in the past.

"Nathan says you've been around a bit," she offered almost hesitantly. "He mean Vietnam?"

Tripp found himself suddenly in a silent battle...with himself. A private man who had locked things away for years—a man who had compartmentalized his life and thrown away the keys—now wanted to share it all with a woman sitting next to him on a mountainside. A woman who'd been in his life for less than a week. The private man began to lose...slowly.

"Vietnam," said Tripp, "then college. Came back here and went to school. Then east—Chicago, Washington, New York." Tripp smiled quietly to himself. "When I was a kid, I thought Chicago was next to New York. Looked pretty close on the map."

"What did you do?"

"Reporter," said Tripp. "Newspapering."

"Sounds romantic."

"For a while. Then it all starts to blur together. Words and deadlines. Life on the end of a telephone." He paused, remembering that life. It seemed a long time ago and a long way removed from this woman and this hillside.

"Travel a lot?"

"Home address was an airplane...seat twenty-nine C," said Tripp. "Yeah, I traveled a lot. What about you?"

"Seattle," said Kathy. "And then a lot of other cities. My dad was in the service, so we never really set down any roots. We'd be in one place a couple of years, then move on.''

Tripp nodded. He'd known people in that life—and felt sorry for them. They never stayed, so they never committed. To anything. When things got difficult they just moved on. Confused wanderers with eyes perpetually trained on the horizon, they never noticed the scenery.

"Then school—back east," Kathy continued. "A job in Boston. Pretty drab...pretty predictable. Spent about half my life chasing a degree. The other half trying to figure out what to do with it. Academic gypsy." She laughed self-consciously and tasted her wine. "So, seat twenty-nine C, huh?"

Tripp picked at his sandwich. "Life became just one big airport with a telephone attached."

"So you came back here?"

"Did it for twenty years," Tripp said. "Then, one day I just sort of couldn't do it anymore. Sat down to write a piece"—he smiled—"and it seemed familiar. Turns out I'd written almost exactly the same story fifteen years before. Different names...but same story."

"Guess they call it burnout?"

"Not really burnout. Just kind of suckout. Like everything's been sucked out of the process." Tripp was quiet for a time. "You get in thinking you'll make a difference. And you get out twenty years later realizing no one actually makes a difference. World continues to spin. And you finally figure out after awhile that you're barely a blip on the screen."

"So you came home and started ranching?"

Tripp laughed out loud. "Sorry," he said, "but what I do isn't really ranching. I live on a ranch, but that's about as close as it gets. I just sort of hole up there."

"But you have horses?" said Kathy, goading him good-naturedly.

"Since last fall only," answered Tripp. "And they're barely horses."

"They're sweet," said Kathy. "Can we give them all sugar next time?"

"You bet, lady," said Tripp. "Consider this a standing invitation to feed and water my livestock any time the urge strikes. Take a load off my poor overburdened shoulders." Tripp had meant it as a joke, but Kathy clouded over.

"Are you any closer, Ben?"

"Don't know what to tell you," answered Tripp. He lay back and stared up through the pine boughs. "Things got a little more complicated last night. Some jerk beaned me. Tried to torch my barn with me in it."

Kathy started as if she'd been slapped. "Ben," she said, "somebody went after you? What happened? Are you okay? Why didn't you tell me?"

Tripp filled her in on the attack and the fire. "Not a big deal. Handled it. But it's a worry. Obvious now your car wreck was no accident. They went after you, then they went after me."

"You're okay?" Doubt in her dark eyes and concern in her elegant face.

Tripp smiled. "A little lumpier than before, but okay. Just don't see how it plays, how it fits in."

They watched the scenery for a while, Tripp thinking about the fire in the shed, Kathy glancing worriedly his way from time to time.

"There's nothing obvious about anything so

far," said Tripp at length. "But I've talked to his professors. And there's maybe some odd conflicts in the stories."

"Like what?"

Tripp outlined it for her: both Crossley and Donner coming up with different reasons for it, but both saying that Grady had been slacking off.

"I don't know what to say," Kathy answered. "I know he was so busy that it was tough to arrange a time to chat."

"That's a hole," said Tripp. "And holes intrigue me." Tripp thought back to the politician he had nailed. A man with presidential ambitions. A man whose picture had been on magazines. The holes about him didn't fit at first, didn't say anything. But there had been more and more until they were like the dots that make up a picture in a newspaper. One or two alone, and you have no idea what the picture is. Dozens and dozens of dots, and an image begins to emerge. In the politician's case, an image of absolute corruption.

Tripp had been watching the meadow below them. Suddenly he put his fingers to his lips and gestured for Kathy to be quiet. She followed his gaze.

Off in front of them, perhaps two hundred yards—just where the meadow merged into the slope of the mountain—the heavy antlered head of an elk had pushed through a curtain of willows. They could clearly see its wary eyes searching up the hillside toward them. Tripp and Kathy sat frozen.

After a minute or so the elk emerged fully from the willows. Its antlers moved in an exaggerated arc as the big animal swung its head from side to side. Its reddish brown coat glistened in the sun as it moved unhurriedly across the narrow clearing. The elk turned and seemed to gaze back up the slope to where the two humans sat. Then it was gone into a tall curtain of brush.

"That was spectacular," whispered Kathy, her cheeks flushed and her eyes shining.

Tripp nodded. "Probably has a herd around here close by."

"Is that common?" said Kathy. "I mean, to see an actual deer out walking around like that? Just like it was on a Sunday stroll. Didn't seem to mind us a bit."

"Not a deer, an elk," said Tripp. "And, yeah, there're plenty around these days. Saw a herd down by Bowen's the other day crossing the highway. Had cars stopped for a quarter of a mile."

"Unbelievable. That's the most remarkable thing I think I've ever seen." Her eyes were bright. They both watched the meadow, but nothing else appeared. At length, Tripp broke the silence.

"You called Donner and Crossley? How'd they seem?"

"Pleasant. Concerned."

"Talk to anybody else?"

"Just the police," said Kathy. "And they wouldn't help."

"John Hunt?"

"Scott had mentioned the name, but that's all. I didn't try to talk with him."

"Corry Sound?"

"What's that?"

"A woman Grady knows."

"He never mentioned her."

"The time sequence?" said Tripp. "Your best bet is he disappeared on that Saturday? The 23rd?"

Kathy said they'd had a lunch date for Saturday the 23rd, that she'd called him the day before, and that he said he'd be working all day Friday, but Saturday was good.

"So you talked to him on Friday?"

"On the phone. And then I went to the student union center on Saturday for lunch and he didn't show up. I waited about an hour, but he didn't show. Tried calling him both at the school and home, but couldn't get him."

Quiet for a time, then Tripp: "I've got to tell you, on top of everything else that's happened, the break-in at your place is bothering me a lot. It's obviously related in some way to Scott's disappearance. But why a month after? That's what I don't get. And why didn't they take anything? What were they looking for? You're sure nothing's missing? I mean, did Scott ever give you anything, or anything like that?"

"Give me anything?"

"Like jewelry or notes or anything like that?"

"Not really," she said. "He's as poor as a church mouse. Maybe a couple of books, some rocks he liked. Stuff like that, but nothing important."

"Anything missing?"

"Nathan and I checked things and it looked okay. I mean, there wasn't anything obvious missing."

"Maybe we could look again?" offered Tripp. "Something you might have overlooked? Maybe stop by and take another look around? Maybe this afternoon?"

"We can," said Kathy, but there was reluctance in her voice. "We can look. But I tell you there's nothing gone." She looked away and Tripp had the feeling something was being left unsaid.

"There's something else?" he asked gently.

She didn't answer at once. When she finally did, it was in a voice so soft as to be almost a whisper. "I don't know if the break-in's related to this whole thing." She looked off toward the mountains. "It's not the first break-in, actually. It's the first time here in Montana, but it happened once before—back east." Tripp remained silent.

"I had a problem with a student there. In Boston. A lost soul of a boy I'd made friends with. I guess he mistook friendship for something else." Kathy looked at Tripp. "You know the kind of thing I mean?"

Tripp nodded, silently recalling Donner's comment about the woman attracting stray puppies.

"Anyway, I guess it became a sort of compulsion for the boy. He started following me around campus, things like that. He'd run into me in stores and at school. He always pretended it was accidental, but I knew it wasn't."

Kathy played with a small orange wildflower. Tripp could tell it was a tough topic.

"And I started getting weird phone calls. Not dirty or anything. But the phone'd ring and I'd pick it up and there'd be nobody there. I mean, you could tell that somebody was there, but they wouldn't say anything. I knew it was the boy. And that's about the time my apartment got broken into. I was living in an apartment in Boston then and had gone to Seattle for a week. And it was the same thing.

Somebody broke in while I was gone. It had to be the boy. Nosed through everything but didn't take anything. The same thing as the other night.''

"You confront him?"

"No," said Kathy, looking away. "No, I didn't. I mean, I'd already gotten the job out here and knew I'd be moving and everything. So I just kind of lay low. And then I moved and it was over."

Tripp thought about the service brat moving from town to town. No roots, no permanency, and no resolve to stay and see out the rough parts. Easier to run than to confront head-on.

"But I guess maybe it wasn't over," Kathy said quietly, a note of resignation in her voice. Tripp looked at her. "The kid followed me," she said. "Compulsive behavior, I guess. I was walking across campus one day last fall and there he was. On the sidewalk in front of me. He'd transferred out here. I almost lost it."

"Has it been the same? The phone calls and the spying?"

"Not really. I mean, I don't think the boy has been following me around the way he did in Boston. I see him once in a while on campus and he looks at me. But it's not the same behavior." She paused and Tripp got the feeling again she'd left something out.

"Different behavior?"

"Letters." She uttered the word in a kind of tired sigh. "I guess it was late last year I started getting letters. Poems, actually. Nothing dirty or anything like that. Just poems. Pretty awful poetry, but poetry. They were always typed and signed, and I think the boy was pretty proud of them. He'd mail

them in those big manila envelopes, and I suspect
he did that so the pages wouldn't have to be
folded.'' She sighed. ''I thought it was behind me.
But it wasn't.''

''You report it?''

''Report what?'' she said tiredly. ''That a boy has
a crush on an old teacher and sends her poems?''

''Still getting them?''

''Once in awhile. I don't even look at them anymore. I just put them in the closet and forget it.''

''You save 'em?'' said Tripp.

''I don't really know why. Maybe as evidence if
it turned ugly. But it hasn't.''

''And you think he's the one who broke into your
house this time?'' asked Tripp, realizing that the
case had widened substantially. Another dot had
presented itself.

''I suppose. It's the same thing. Nothing taken.
Somebody just going through my things.''

''Does this kid''—Tripp paused—''sorry, what's
this kid's name?''

''Vernon Wells.''

''Does this Wells kid know Grady?''

''I don't know,'' said Kathy. ''Well, I suppose
he knows who he is. I mean, if he's followed me
at all I'm sure he's seen me with Scott. Even if he
hasn't followed me, I suppose he'd have seen us
around.'' She looked at Tripp dubiously. ''Wells
and Grady? I've thought of it, wondered about it. I
just don't know. God, can you imagine if that's the
case…if Wells did something to Grady over me?''
The woman rubbed her eyes. ''I don't know if I
could live with that.''

''I'll talk to him,'' said Tripp, wondering silently

why she hadn't mentioned the boy before now. Kathy seemed to read his thoughts.

"I was embarrassed, Ben," she said. "It's like it was dirty or something."

"And you felt like you were to blame for it." Tripp meant it as a question, but it came out more a declaration of fact. "I'll talk to the kid."

"I want to go home, Ben," Kathy said wearily.

"Yeah, it's getting late."

"Not to Bowen's. I want to go home."

"Kathy—" Tripp began, but she interrupted him, an edge of anger in her voice.

"We were all panicked when I discovered I'd been broken into. I think, with the stress of the wreck and Scott and all of that, we jumped, and maybe a little too high. I think Wells is probably behind the break-in. And he's not a danger, Ben."

The instinct to flee, thought Tripp to himself— *it's stronger in the woman than the instinct to fight.* "Look," he said aloud, his voice firm and commanding, "something's most definitely dangerous out there. I don't know if Grady's dead or alive. I don't even know if your wreck up Pattee Canyon was an accident or intentional. But I do know somebody came after me and tried to kill me. That's real, and this thing isn't just gonna slide away. And running from it isn't gonna solve it."

Kathy's eyes had teared up. "I'm so out of my element, Ben. And it sounds dumb, but I feel so incredibly helpless." She brushed at a tear.

Tripp put his hand on her arm. "Wrong feeling, Kathy. You're not alone on this thing. And you're not helpless. We're gonna figure this one out."

Tripp dug into his pocket. "Thought you might

be missing this,'' he said, holding out his hand. In it the small gold earring.

Kathy closed her fist around it. Her eyes teared and she turned away. ''Does this have an end, Ben?''

Tripp touched her shoulder. ''It has an end, Kathy. It has an end.''

TEN

KATHY TURNED the key in the front door and Tripp pushed in past her. The front room he remembered so well, with its books and trinket-covered mantel, seemed draped in gloom. A stale, mousy scent filled the air. Kathy edged in behind him.

"Same little house," she said. "Maybe this'll help." She opened a Venetian blind and light poured in. She fanned the air in front of her face with her good hand. "Like nobody's been here for years. Leave the front door open and let's air it out."

Tripp wedged the door open with a book.

"Things look all right," she said, surveying the room. "Nothing's obviously missing."

"You said Grady gave you some things," said Tripp. "I think you said books, rocks, things like that."

Kathy nodded and moved to the bookshelf. "This," she said, offering a hard bound book to Tripp. "History of the West. I'd told Scott I was interested in the West and he showed up one day with this. Think he bought it new."

Tripp paged through it. Lewis and Clark, William Powell, Fremont.

"And this one," said Kathy. "Wolfgang Puck's cookbook." She smiled as she scanned its glossy cover. "I don't think Scott ever realized I don't cook."

Tripp inspected the mantel. Small, silver-framed photos of Kathy with friends. One on a beach, another in a motorboat, Kathy waving, smiling. A black-and-white photo of a man and a woman together. The man had on a uniform. A half dozen or so rocks lay haphazardly among the pictures.

"From Scott," she said. "Fossils, I guess. I think he was pretty proud of them. Wanted me to have some." She picked up a rock about the size of an orange and inspected it. "Old, old bone. He told me the names of these things, but I've forgotten them." She set it back amid the other rocks and straightened a photo, stepping back to admire the mantel from a distance.

"Important to Scott?" asked Tripp.

Kathy nodded. "He was proud of all of them. You know, they're just rocks to me, but the way he made a fuss over them, you could tell he was awfully proud of them. His small treasures."

The two moved into the kitchen and Kathy opened more blinds. The room was tidy, the drying rack in the sink empty of dishes. She opened the refrigerator and lunged back theatrically.

"Now that's gross." She laughed. "That milk could walk out of there." Tripp was peering in over her shoulder. "And look at that lettuce. Gross." She pointed toward the other end of the narrow kitchen. "Door leads into the backyard. Bedroom and office down the other way. You'll see. Help yourself." She turned back to attack the refrigerator.

The office was midway down the hall in an alcove cut between the bathroom and bedroom. A desk with a green-shaded piano lamp, a wooden chair, more shelves of books, and a short filing cabinet. Tripp opened a desk drawer and idly paged through receipts and some school reports, a tumble of wrinkled travel advertisements, and a stack of bank envelopes held together with a rubber band.

After awhile Kathy came up behind him. "Anything jumping out?"

"Not a thing. Actually, I figured out on about the second drawer that I didn't know what I was looking for. So no, not a thing." Tripp gestured toward the hallway. "Bedroom?"

A queen-size bed under an Indian-looking quilt took up most of the room. To one side an elaborate oak bureau with a large mirror was hung with enameled and feathered Mardi Gras masks. On the other side another tall case of books next to a narrow closet.

"Nothing missing in all this?"

Kathy shook her head. "Just clothes and books in here, and it's all here, I suppose. I mean, I didn't look at every book. Probably wouldn't know if one was missing. But there's nothing obvious."

"Jewelry."

"Cheap stuff," said Kathy, opening a hand-tooled wooden box on the marble top of the bureau. She pulled out a heavy silver necklace and, turning to the mirror, laid it over her chest. "This is about the best thing here. Silver and turquoise. Indian. From my mother. But it's obviously here."

"Wells' letters? You mind?"

Kathy squatted down in the closet doorway, straining around to one side and digging behind a rack of hanging dresses and skirts. "Need to clean this one of these days," she said in a voice muffled by cotton and nylon. "Got it." She backed up pull-

ing a cardboard box along the floor. A couple of
errant shoes and small dust balls fell to the side as
she pushed it into the room. "Sorry, but I'm obviously not all that domestic," she said, standing up
and trying to blow a strand of hair from her face.
Tripp knelt to examine the letters.

"All here?" he asked as he rifled through about
a dozen manila envelopes.

"Didn't look," she said. "Think there's about
ten of them."

Tripp pulled out the nearest one and read the envelope. "This month's postmark. Just got it?"

"It was here when I got back from Denver."

Tripp broke the seal and pulled out a single sheet
of typing paper. The printing looked like it was
from a computer. A single word centered in large
type at the top of the page: *Madding.* Just beneath
it the name Vernon Wells. Below that six lines:

Black on the inside of nothing,
Not even shadow to build form.
Screams that bleed to silence
In a cavern with no echoes.
Walls grotesque to touch
Cry out at the pushing crowd.

Tripp sat back on his heels and tucked the paper
into the envelope.

"Pretty awful, isn't it?" said Kathy behind him.
"Weird."

"Yeah, weird. They're all like that. Dark, nasty.
Brutish is a pretty good word. Maybe spooky's better."

Tripp dug through the box, reading more poems

as he went. All had a dark-toned edge, most spoke of caves or blackened tunnels. One talked about a blood-edged scimitar over a pallid neck.

Tripp got up and moved to the single window. The wood was shaved and nicked where someone had forced a knife or shiv to spring the lock. He ran his finger along the edge, managing to impale himself with a small, sharp splinter. He barked, jamming the finger into his mouth.

"Problem?"

"Dry wood," Tripp mouthed from around his finger. "Can't trust it. Great carpenter, aren't I?"

Tripp opened the window lock and pulled up the lower pane. Outside a small backyard. Beyond it the alley. "So somebody broke in when you were in the hospital?"

Kathy moved to his side and looked out. "You dropped me off on Tuesday, remember? Then I went out for the count. Slept through to Wednesday." Tripp lowered the window. "Then I guess I was sort of in a daze. I tried cleaning things up a bit. Air them out. Opened the doors and then the windows. When I got to this one, it was odd. It was already open. I don't do that. I mean, I never"— she emphasized the word—"never leave windows unlocked. Too many years in big cities. Then I saw the marks and called Nathan."

Tripp sat on the edge of the bed. "And you're sure it happened when you were in the hospital? Couldn't have happened when you were in Denver?"

"Well, yeah, I'm pretty sure." But her voice was tentative. "I mean, I cleaned when I got home from Denver. I aired the place out. And I always open the windows when I do that. I mean..." Kathy lapsed into silence and Tripp watched her face. She turned again to the window, unlocked it, moved the pane up, then lowered it. "Ben, I'm sorry. But now I just don't remember. I don't remember if I ever even looked at this window when I came home from Denver. I always keep the blind closed. I would have opened the blind if I opened the window. But I honestly don't remember if I opened the window." She turned back to Tripp. "It could have been any time."

ELEVEN

THE SUN WAS NEARLY SET and the trees along the river cast long blue shadows as Tripp and Kathy pulled into Bowen's that afternoon. Bowen was at the porch table banging on something with his fist, a look of determination on his face. "Catch any fish, Mr. Walton?" he called out as the two unloaded the pickup.

"Didn't even try." Tripp laughed. "Struck gold instead."

"You should see this old camp," said Kathy. "It's beautiful up there."

Bowen only grinned. "Sun's well over the yardarm," he said. "Join me for grog on the fantail?"

"What's all this?" said Kathy, inspecting the pieces arrayed in front of Bowen.

"Equipment maintenance." He laughed. "We professional"—he emphasized the word—"professional fisherman keep our gear immaculate. So when the fish of a lifetime hits, we're ready."

"And he does mean immaculate," added Tripp. "Fish like that'd be the immaculate conception for old Bones here. I'll take a drink."

"First a shower," said Kathy. "Mining gold's dirty work, even if it's just placer and not hard rock." She'd exaggerated the words and made a face at Tripp.

"You spent the day giving this fine lady geology

lessons?'' said Bowen in mock astonishment. "The rocks, Mr. Boulder, are in your head.''

Bowen followed Kathy inside and reappeared with two tumblers of ice water and whiskey. The two men arranged themselves in the porch's ragged easy chairs. "Good day?'' asked Bowen, nodding toward the house and the woman in it.

"Good day, mostly,'' said Tripp. "Nice lady. Good picnic. Thanks.''

"Wants out of here pretty badly,'' said Bowen. "Don't suppose we can keep her if she decides to go.''

"Think she'll give us a day or two,'' said Tripp, explaining what Kathy had told him about Vernon Wells.

"Major A-one suspect, sounds like to me,'' said Bowen when Tripp had fallen silent. "Since we've probably got two or three crimes going on here, I guess we can probably award one to him.''

"Make that three or four crimes,'' said Tripp. He told Bowen about the crack on the head and the burning shop.

Bowen's initial look of disbelief turned to a shallow, teasing grin. "So you almost got your stamps canceled, huh? Gonna have to be a little more careful, Ben old boy. They say most accidents happen around the home. Any ideas who?''

"None. Didn't even see part of him. Just felt the business end of a pretty good swing.''

Off toward the river a wedge of ducks circled to land.

"A couple of things sort of jump to mind,'' said Bowen after awhile. "First one is, that's a very sweet lady in there. Sweet to me, sweet on you.''

Bowen looked for reaction, but Tripp kept his face blank. Kathy had come to haunt his thoughts. He missed her when he was away from her—and felt silly about that later—and realized he was happiest when he was around her. But the whole issue was shaded with ambivalence. Though his divorce was well in the past, he remained gun-shy about the idea of relationships.

"Second thing is," said Bowen to his friend's silence, "second thing is, seems to me things are kind of scattered at this point. Maybe we need to back it up and see how it all plays?"

Tripp only nodded.

"There's no corpus delicti, as they say," observed Bowen. "And that's a difficulty because it tends to cloud reasoning. Show me a body and I'll show you who done it. But no body."

"Right. No body," said Tripp automatically, but his thoughts were on Wells and the poetry. It felt ominous to Tripp, dangerous. He wondered if the mind that could write that was the kind of mind that could kill a woman.

"But," said Bowen, surveying his reel with a squinted, suspicious eye, "but we do have a series of events. Maybe unrelated, maybe intertwined. How 'bout a dance, partner? If you lead, I'll follow."

Tripp forced his mind away from the dark poems. "Right, guess it's time for a little tango here." He sipped at his drink. "We've got a disappeared guy who doesn't usually disappear. Mildly suspicious. Second, we've got the wreck. Suspicious again. Maybe an accident. Maybe attempted murder. Circumstances tend to indicate accident. Timing points toward murder. Then things thicken up a bit. A break-in and then last night's little nastiness." Tripp watched as a handful of ducks broke out of the main V and glided in toward a quiet finger of the river. "And the break-in at Kathy's just gotten a little more nebulous."

Bowen looked up questioningly.

"Weird," said Tripp. "Can't pin down the timing of that as exactly as I thought we could."

"Not during the hospital?"

"Can't tell. We went over there this afternoon. And she can't remember now if she ever even looked at that window after she got back from Denver."

"Not good. So it could have been any time?"

"'Fraid so."

"Still a crime, partner."

"No doubt about that," said Tripp. "Still a crime. But I can't see where it fits anything. Just nothing clear."

Tripp lapsed into silence, trying to piece it together. The disappearance, the car wreck, the break-in, the attempt on him: He'd thought they were linear, all falling into place one after another. But uncertain now. Did someone force his way into Kathy's apartment before he tried killing her? Discover something there, decide she had to die? Or force his way in after he thought he'd killed her? Break in when he knew she wouldn't be around to object?

"Got ourselves a real mess here." Tripp seemed to be talking now as much to himself as to Bowen. "And it seems to be getting bigger." He watched his friend tinker with the reel. "Wonder if we might not also have just a bit of coincidence banging around in all this, too.'' He recalled Kathy's conviction that the most recent break-in was just like the first one, the one committed by Vernon Wells.

"Seems to me," said Bowen, glancing up briefly as he tried to load a balky spring into the reel, "seems to me that if you're gonna earn your salary, you can't take anything for granted. Have to assume it's all crime until you're proven wrong. Then you can walk around introducing yourself as Ben Tripp, investigator of really pretty amazing coincidences. Quite a deal," Bowen said, chuckling.

They were quiet for a time, Bowen lost in the reel, Tripp lost in the case. From within the old house they could hear the shower come on. Kathy was whistling—off tune.

"Okay," Tripp said finally, "let's give ourselves some more assumables—just for the pure joy of it. Assume Grady's dead. I've stowed his body over there in the root cellar.''

"The root cellar?" said Bowen, looking up.

"Assumptions," Tripp reminded him. "How much whiskey have you had?"

"Okay, Grady's dead and he's in my root cellar," said Bowen. "No, it's this mechanical marvel here in front of me. Got it all back together and there's one extra part. This little ratchet thing." He held it up for Tripp to look at, then studied it close to his eyes. "Don't think I've ever seen this thing. You ever see a part like this in a reel?"

Tripp shook his head.

"Bad deal here," said Bowen. "How do you suppose that happened? Nuts." He tossed the part down on the table and took an extralong pull from the whiskey glass.

"Stay with me," said Tripp. "So Grady's dead, and now our girl goes out looking for Grady and somebody tries to kill her. Then I go out looking for that person and somebody tries to take me out." Tripp looked across to his friend.

"So whoever killed Grady has tried to kill the somebodies looking," said Bowen. "Seems reasonable enough. Doesn't answer the why worth a nickel, but it's reasonable enough." He was looking off toward the river. "They say fishin's pretty good right now. Guy through here the other day says they pulled a five-pound rainbow from the Blackfoot."

"One of the rules is," said Tripp, "one of the rules is that the victim always knows the killer. Or maybe that's just in the killings the police manage to solve."

"Can't say it's been much of a year for me, though," said Bowen. The two men might as well have been in different counties. "I caught that nice brown on the Flathead, but you never believed it 'cause I threw it back. Gonna carry a camera from now on when I fish."

"But if it's true most of the time," said Tripp thoughtfully, "maybe it stands up this time. Grady probably knew his killer—if he's dead. So do we now know everybody Grady knows—or knew?"

"You know how they fish in the South?" said Bowen. "They just throw out garbage on a string, and those fish'll hit it. Bass'll hit the weirdest stuff."

"Garbage on a string?" asked Tripp vaguely, glancing at his friend.

"Six-inch rubber frogs painted purple that whir

and thump," said Bowen, banging on the reel again. "And those fish'll hit 'em."

"Tough to figure out everybody a person knows or comes into contact with," said Tripp. "I read somewhere that everybody has a circle of about fifty or sixty acquaintances that they know and do business with."

"It's almost criminal," said Bowen. "They'll catch fifty or sixty bass in a morning." Bowen shook his head sadly. "And they use boats. Has to be a pretty stupid fish."

"There're the people Grady lives around," said Tripp, recalling the good-looking, vacuous girl at the apartment house and the skinny man. "Have to go back there when more people are around."

"Need to go back to the Flathead," said Bowen. "Gonna tie a little purple on the end of a Royal Coachman. See if that works. A bass fisherman wouldn't know a dry fly if it snagged him in the butt."

"And we've got to get a better handle on the other significant players," said Tripp. "Crossley, Donner, maybe Hunt. Obviously Vernon Wells. And the girl. Corry Sound."

Bowen rose ponderously to freshen their drinks. His mind seemed to have switched off fishing when he returned.

"Motive, Sherlock," he said. "You have to think motive."

"Unknown," answered Tripp. "Crossley, the great dinosaur slayer, pretty much owes his career to Grady. So why knock the boy off if he's your bread ticket? Maybe some professional jealousy— or a turf fight we know nothing about?"

"Reasonable."

"Donner," said Tripp. "The good Howard Donner. Initially close to the boy, then distant." Tripp thought about his visit to Donner's fancy house on the hill. "Maybe a man with something to hide. Maybe not. We can't forget he's in the same department, in the same business. Maybe another turf fight. But no obvious motive."

"Puget Sound?"

Tripp groaned. "Corry Sound. Between those mugs you give me and lousing up names, it's a wonder I have any sanity left."

Bowen wrinkled his heavy brow in mock pain. "Gettin' testy in your old age, aren't you, pardner? Love life must be pretty bare, judging by your temper. Hope you're better at that than you are at fishing."

Tripp shrugged. "Okay, Corry Sound. Complete blank, complete unknown. Maybe significant in Grady's life, maybe not. Still have to find her to find any of that out."

"And our new addition to the big happy family?" said Bowen. "Old what's-his-name, Indian Wells?"

"Vernon Wells. Maybe a man with a motive— maybe not. Maybe hates Grady for moving in on what he considers his lady. Jealous rage, that sort of thing. Takes him in an alley and beans him on the head. Dead Grady. But why go after Kathy? No sense there."

Bowen nodded. "You been fishing at all this summer?"

"And John Hunt," said Tripp, ignoring him. "Fellow graduate student, fellow traveler. Always a step or two behind. Maybe professional jealousy. Lose Grady and step into the winner's circle.''

"Check where they were on the 23rd and last Monday night and then last night," said Bowen. "If you can't find motive, you might be able to pin down opportunity.''

"Already did with Donner," said Tripp. "He says he was at a meeting in Idaho on the 23rd.''

"Crossley?"

"Problematical," said Tripp. "Pretty far away. Talked about being at a meeting or something early this week. I don't know where he was on the 23rd. I actually forgot to ask. Great detective work. But I'll check it. And tough for him to have been in my barn last night with a Zippo. I met him Thursday in Shelby. Would've had to hurry to get here first.''

"Hunt?"

"Don't know."

"And our young obsessive-compulsive, Mr. Wells?" said Bowen.

"A blank page at this point," said Tripp. Bowen went back to tinkering with his reel. Kathy whistled from inside the store. And Tripp thought about getting to know more about Grady's small circle of friends.

TWELVE

Instead of taking the road up Pattee Canyon that night and heading for the ranch, Tripp made a detour north and within fifteen minutes was parked along a quiet residential street at the base of the mountain on which Howard Donner's house was perched. It was still early—before eight—but the houses along the street seemed lifeless, their privacies conducted behind drawn curtains and shuttered glass.

From where he had parked, Tripp could see both Donner's house protruding over the slope of the mountain and the switchback road leading from it. A soft wind blew from the south. A dog barked in staccato warning at some unseen threat from a backyard.

A little after nine and Tripp realized with a start that he'd been nodding. The lights were off all around the Donner split-level, and headlights were making their way down the zigzagging road. Tripp started up the pickup and huddled down behind the wheel.

Shortly the red Corvette of the night before emerged onto the flat of the street ahead, and Tripp could just make out Donner's shorn head in the gloom of a streetlight. Tripp gave the car enough time to get well ahead and then followed.

Donner's first stop was a liquor store. From a half block away, Tripp could see that Donner had dressed in black for whatever the occasion was: a black long-sleeved shirt, black slacks, black shoes. Donner went directly to the wine racks, selected a bottle, paid, and was on his way again. Tripp fell in well to the rear.

Back into residential streets for only a few blocks before the Corvette pulled into the driveway of a large house. Tripp pulled up short and turned off on a side street, parking the truck out of sight.

As he hurried around the corner on foot, Tripp could see Donner at the opened front door being hugged by a woman in a long dress. Sounds of laughter and music spilled out into the night. The woman laced her arm through Donner's and walked him inside. The door closed and the party's high notes were replaced by the steady beat of a stereo bass.

Tripp walked casually past on the sidewalk, glancing through the two large brightly lit picture windows that fronted the street. About two dozen people were scattered through two rooms. A few couples were dancing. Most were just talking and drinking. A black-clad waiter threaded through the throng with a tray of food. He couldn't spot Donner in the crush.

Tripp made his way back to the truck and moved it to a spot in deep shadow down the street from the house.

The party continued to roar as Tripp played with the radio in the darkened cab. Three stations in town and his choices were all country-western. At ten he listened to the hourly news from New York. Midnight in New York. He wondered what some of his old newspaper friends there were doing right then.

Thought about the day five years before when he'd quit. A dreary, snowy day in Manhattan. Steam oozing from the streets. The overheated lobby of his building. Guard who never remembered his face checking IDs. Elevator up. Curious eyes glancing furtively. One well-delivered, heartfelt fist to the chin of the managing editor. Down the elevator and gone.

Tripp absently rubbed a knuckle and watched the house. At 11:30 people started to trickle out. Midnight, and Donner emerged on the arm of the same woman who had greeted him. An air kiss as they hugged, and then Donner left alone. Tripp waited a few beats and fell in behind, once again well to the rear.

Donner's route led not toward his mountain aerie but across town toward the university district. At length, Donner turned north and then picked up the freeway headed east out of town. Tripp stayed well back, following the dual taillights in the night.

Donner took the first exit. A small, gritty lumber town throttled by steep mountains on one side, the river on the other—a freakish orange cast to the black night sky from the lights of a paper mill along the river. The frontage road was deserted and Tripp dropped back even farther as Donner cruised slowly through the shuttered town and down a stretch of blacktop. Tripp watched the taillights as the professor pulled into a sprawling truck stop that paralleled the freeway—a handful of semis parked under the lit pump bays, a line of men at a lunch counter, hunched backs toward the broad glass windows, more semis idling off in the shadows, their running lights glowing like some awkward diesel parody of Christmas.

Tripp watched as Donner made his way inside the diner. The black-clad professor walked down the line of men at the counter and disappeared around a side hall. A minute or so later he reappeared and took a seat at the counter. Tripp could clearly make out a waitress as she leaned over to take Donner's order. She turned, poured a cup of coffee, and set it before him. Donner dug into the pocket of his black pants and placed something on the counter. The waitress swept it away and moved on down the line of men. Donner took a sip from his cup, set it back down, and turned on the swivel seat, looking out through the windows toward the line of idling semis. Tripp shrank back in his seat, hoping he'd parked far enough back that Donner wouldn't notice the pickup.

Donner turned to his coffee, appeared to taste it, and then rose. He disappeared around a corner hallway and emerged from the gloom at the side of the building, headed back toward the parking lot.

At his car the professor turned, surveyed the parked trucks, then climbed in and cruised slowly out. Tripp ducked down as the headlights swung past him and then did a quick U-turn and picked up the tail.

Tripp followed well behind as the path of earlier was repeated in reverse: back through the sleeping town, past the garish stain of the pulp mill, along the frontage road, and then onto the freeway, where Donner kicked in a burst of speed. Tripp's old pickup was no match for the Corvette. He watched and cursed as the taillights disappeared before him around a corner of the canyon.

When he finally made his way to the base of the mountain and the shuttered street where he'd started the tail, Tripp could see that the lights were on again at the Donner perch. As he pulled up to watch, the living room lights dimmed and went out. A light came on on the floor above and shone for maybe two minutes before it too went out and Donner's house was swallowed in mountain blackness.

Tripp sat for a time along the darkened street digesting what he'd seen, trying to fit it into the odd dance of human behavior that was circling his search for Scott Grady. At length, he started the pickup and headed up the canyon toward the ranch.

THIRTEEN

TRIPP'S MOOD paralleled the weather Sunday morning—gray and snarly. Thunder echoed off the mountains as he tended the horses and did general cleanup around the barn and the feedlot. He thought about making it a fishing day—cloudy skies brought the fish up out of the deep runs, and the trout could be hitting hard on dry flies. But Kathy Sullivan pushed at the back of his mind. He took a shower instead.

Mid-morning, and Tripp was back at the university, this time at the large main library. At the public phones he fed a line of quarters into a number he had once known so well that he remembered it still five years later. An automated computer voice demanded another dollar fifty. The phone rang at least ten times before it was answered.

"*Times*, help you?" said a man hurriedly.

"National," said Tripp.

"Hold one," the man said curtly. Tripp was surprised to find that he was actually nervous talking to the desk—the same desk he'd dealt with daily for almost fifteen years. He imagined the scene in the newsroom: early Sunday afternoon, coffee cups scattered around from the Saturday shift, and reporters beginning to filter back in to put the Monday bulldog edition out. Thinnest edition of the week. A skeleton crew. The suits and ties came in on Monday.

A click: "Siebens." A woman's voice. Matter-of-fact.

"Tripp," he said simply.

A pause he could have driven a truck through.

"Tripp," said the voice at length. "Tripp? Tripp. Let's see. Think I used to know a Tripp once. Pretty good reporter. Nah, I'm thinking about somebody else. This Tripp was a bum. He died." A pause.

"How are you, P. K.?" said Tripp, grinning into the phone.

"Or he ran off to the woods somewhere. Better if he died."

"Hi, P. K."

"Last I heard, this Tripp bum had gone out West. 'Get a little spread, run a few head,' or some such trash."

"You haven't changed much, P. K."

"Home, home on the range." He could hear the smile in her voice.

"Hi, P. K."

"Hi, Tripp," said the woman. "*The* Ben Tripp? Gotta have some ID, buster."

"Hope your teeth rot, P. K."

"That's it," she said, trying to sit on her laughter. "Nastiest man ever to win a Pulitzer. Pulitzer Prize for purple prose, wasn't it? Tripp. How are you, Ben Tripp?"

"Makin' do," he said. "How's life in the exit lane?"

"Same old same old."

"Still in national?" he asked. The paper's two main news desks were national and foreign. He'd worked national with P. K. Siebens.

"Still here," she said. "Sexist thugs finally had to make me editor." They laughed together: The paper was notorious for its old-boy network.

"Congratulations, P. K."

"Ben Tripp," she said. "My. Three or four years now, huh?"

"Five, actually."

"And you're where—Wyoming, Idaho?"

"Montana."

"Same thing. Writing?"

"Not a word. Working for a living."

"Working for a living? Hmmnot sure that scans. Slip into English, will ya?"

"I actually work for a living. Lift things, you know, and people pay me money." Or horses, thought Tripp, but decided P. K. wouldn't understand.

A beeping on the line and an operator demanded more money. Tripp fed quarters into the machine.

"Obviously a classy operation," said P. K. "They don't have phones in North Dakota?"

"Montana. I need some help."

"Ah, the proverbial touch," said the woman. "Prepare yourself, Ms. Siebens, the man is about to try a finesse."

"No finesse, P. K. You guys still tied into the national crime computer?"

"They finally caught up with you, huh?"

"I need to run a couple of names."

"A story?"

"Favor for a friend."

"Girlfriend, right?" P. K. laughed. "Some things never change. Gimme the names."

Tripp spelled out the full names of Grady, Crossley, Donner, Wells, Sound, and Hunt and gave the woman general age and description on each. "And P. K., pay particular attention to Donner. University professor. Up to something, but I'm not sure what."

"Will do."

"And try a Sullivan, Kathy, probably Katherine. With a K. Thirty-eight or so, female Caucasian, born Seattle. Boston and Montana residences."

"Ah," said P. K., "the lady emerges. You're now joined at the hip with an Irish gang moll, that it?"

"Somebody tried to kill her," said Tripp. "Like to find out why."

P. K.'s voice turned serious. "I'll run 'em, Tripp. Take an hour or so. Where do I call you?"

"I'll call you. And thanks, P. K. I owe you one."

"You owe me a million, Tripp. And I'll collect if I ever make it to Utah."

Tripp hung up and tried directory assistance for Wells, Vernon. No listing.

Asking directions, Tripp made his way to a tomb-like room in the library's basement and found the news archives computer set back amid a row of microfilm terminals.

The screen blinked to life in front of him, and Tripp entered the library sign-on code and then a complicated series of commands for information on Carl Crossley. The machine thought for a minute and came up with two entries. Tripp hit a key and the first selection appeared.

From the Associated Press
All rights reserved

CAMBRIDGE, *October 13, 1989 (AP)—The dean of Harvard's College of Archaeology an-*

nounced today that a paleontologist noted for his work on the development of theories related to the evolution of dinosaurs will become the new chairman of Harvard's Department of Paleontology.

Tripp scanned through the story. It detailed the Harvard appointment of the scientist who had led the Willow Hills dig. He found Crossley's name in the fourth graph.

Associate director of the Willow Hills operation was Carl Crossley. Professor Crossley teaches at the University of Montana.

Tripp read through the rest of the story. No more mention of Crossley. Short shrift, he realized, for one of the leaders of the excavation.

Tripp hit the proper keys to find the second Crossley reference, but it was just a newspaper rewrite of the wire service story he'd already seen. He tried another entry: "Donner, Howard, Nevada, Montana, Paleontology." The machine took the data bits and began digesting. At length, the computer reported one reference to Donner, Howard. Tripp brought it up. It was a piece from three years before from a Reno newspaper:

RENO—*March 15: A faculty-student review board created to look into charges of illegal drug sales at the University of Nevada, Reno heard closed-door testimony today from a number of students and faculty members.*

> *The board, which was created last Decem-*
> *ber in the wake of the so-called Prolux Affair,*
> *met for nearly six hours. Board members re-*
> *fused to characterize today's testimony, though*
> *one later said that some parts were "explo-*
> *sive."*

Scanning down through the copy, Tripp discovered that the Prolux Affair, as the paper called it,
had begun when a coed charged publicly in the
school paper that one of her professors was selling
drugs to students. Tripp found Donner's name all
but buried near the bottom. It said only that Donner
was one of several professors to appear before the
board and was not himself suspected of any impro-
priety.

Tripp entered a line for Scott Grady. No hits. The
computer couldn't find his name in the public press
since 1985. He keyed in John Hunt. Again nothing.
And nothing for Corrance Sound. He tried "Wells,
Vernon, Boston, Montana." No hits.

He tapped out more letters on the computer:
"Sullivan, Katherine, Boston, Montana, Religions." The cursor blinked as the computer dug
through the database. One entry. Nervously Tripp
keyed it in. It was from the Boston Globe. A long
agate type listing of court proceedings from February 4, 1990. Tripp read down through the listings
until he came on her name:

DIVORCE GRANTED: *Katherine Silvante née*
Sullivan from Michael Anthony Silvante; 4th
District; Judge Lavell Hastings; alienation of
affections; no children.

Tripp stared at the small chapter of a life flashing
on the screen. "Alienation of affections"—legalese

for adultery. And Kathy had sued for the divorce. Caught her husband cheating and divorced him. Good work.

Tripp tried one last entry. "Tripp, Benjamin." The computer came back with 171 hits—bylines from stories he'd written five years before. He turned the machine off.

Back at the pay phone, he called the New York desk. P. K. read out the information from the crime computer: "Crossley, nothing. Donner, nothing. Couldn't even find traffic tickets on the two. As far as the American legal system is concerned, they're clean. Sullivan, same—nothing. Ditto for Sound. Nothing."

P. K. paused, as though reading through notes. "But a hit on your friend Hunt."

Tripp was startled. "Shoot."

"Missoula, Montana, September 1991. Third degree narcotics, cultivation. DEA arrest. Federal judge in the Fifth Circuit dismissed charges. That's it."

"Third degree?" said Tripp.

"An ounce or less, usually," said P. K. "Sheet says cultivation, so it was probably marijuana plants in the garden. Isn't there some federal judge out there throwing all the minor dope cases out? Smokes pot himself or something?"

"Imagine it's the same one."

"These things help?"

"That's it on Hunt?"

"That's it."

"No hits on the others, huh?"

"Not a one. Good story, Tripp?"

"Might be someday," he said. "Right now it's just a favor."

"Nice to hear your voice again, Tripp—after all these years."

"Yours too, P. K.," he said...and couldn't think of anything else to add.

"How's life going out there? Happy?"

"Moderately," said Tripp. "Stayin' busy."

"Married?"

Tripp laughed. "Hardly. What about you? Still?"

"Nope. He found some little thing and was off me like a prom dress. Few bad months, but no more. Can't tell you how good it felt to lose two hundred and forty pounds."

A moment of silence on the line.

"Ever find whatever it was you left for?" P. K. asked. "Any closer, Tripp?"

"Still looking, P. K." He stared at the phone as he hung it back on the receiver.

FOURTEEN

RAIN HAD BEGUN TO DRIFT down by the time Tripp made his way back to the pickup. It had taken him nearly an hour of sorting through the library's class schedules and student directories to find an address for Vernon Wells. He lived in a part of town called the Rattlesnake, a rough name that hid a pricey development along a picturesque mountain-fed stream. Tripp was only mildly surprised that Wells would reside there. Eastern money, he thought to himself. The best kind.

Tripp slowed as he entered the block. The address proved to be a small yellow bungalow set well back off the street. The rear of the property butted into the heavy brush along the creek.

Parking directly in front, Tripp made his way down a narrow flagstone walk and rapped at the door. He could see no signs of life in the house, no car in the driveway. He rapped again. Nothing.

Tripp drove back down through the neighborhood to a convenience store and used its phone to try the Crossley home. No answer. Called Bowen.

"The quest?" asked Bowen.

"Continues," said Tripp. "How's Kathy?"

"Fine, Sherlock. Sleeping. What news there?"

"Not much," said Tripp. "If business isn't too hectic out there, maybe you'd like to take a ride? Thought we might house-sit for Scott Grady for a spell. Fill you in on an interesting ride last night."

"Splendid rainy Sunday activity. Tell me where."

BOWDEN WAS ALREADY there when Tripp pulled up in front of the old house with the weed-covered driveway and the old cars.

"Ah, the good Mr. Locksmith," said Bowen, waving. "I assume you have a key."

"Think the landlady'll probably let us in," said Tripp.

"Don't even bother," said Bowen, proudly holding up a key. "Lovely woman, Mrs. Humble. Promised to take her fishing."

Inside, the apartment was dim and the air stale. Bowen switched on an overhead light and pushed open a curtain. The apartment was really no more than an average-sized room. A neatly made-up bed and a set of drawers hugged one wall; a tidy desk with a computer stood against another. In one corner a stack of homemade shelves bent under a load of rocks and books. A small kitchen area with a sink, a gas range, and an apartment refrigerator filled the other corner.

Bowen opened a door in the wall. "Bathroom."

A door next to the bathroom opened onto a small closet. Tripp turned on its naked bulb. About a dozen shirts and pants were arrayed neatly on hangers hooked over a single aluminum tube. Tripp felt through the pockets of several pairs of blue jeans and khaki dress pants. Nothing. The breast pockets on a couple of heavy wool shirts were empty as well. The only other item was a heavy winter coat with about ten pockets and zippered compartments. Tripp found all of them empty.

Three pairs of shoes were lined up neatly on the floor below the jeans, one of them a scuffed and beaten pair of climbing boots. Next to them, Grady's climbing gear. Tripp knelt and inspected it. The outside pockets of an old rucksack held small chips of rock and fossil and a well-worn pocket knife. Inside the pack, coils of climbing rope and several loops of metal clamps and screws hooked into a kind of harness device. Nothing else, nothing that spoke to Tripp of the vanishing of Scott Grady. Tripp backed out of the closet as Bowen emerged from the bathroom. "Anything?" he asked.

"Well, our boy hadn't packed for a trip, I don't think. All the essentials still in there—razor, toothbrush, shampoo. And I doubt he had spares."

"So," said Tripp, "he hasn't gone on down the road, as one of his professors guessed. Clothes in there"—he gestured toward the closet—"clothes look like everyday stuff. I think they'd be gone if he was in the Bahamas right now. And there's climbing gear in there, too. Climbing gear here means he's not on the rocks out there somewhere."

Tripp pulled open the top drawer of the desk as Bowen started on the dresser.

"School notes," said Tripp, "school notes, schoolbooks, school schedules."

"Underwear," answered Bowen. "And socks and clothes. Not much here."

"And I'm not convinced we'd know important if it jumped out and bit us," said Tripp. He flipped slowly through a stack of graded test papers nearly two inches thick.

At length, he gave up. "Nothing here. Or at least nothing obvious. Nothing actually very personal at all in this stuff. It's mostly school related. Nothing here."

Bowen had begun inspecting the room more generally, kneeling to look under the bed and mattress, sorting through the tiny cabinet over the sink, and rummaging through the refrigerator. He pulled out a tray of ice cubes and knocked them noisily into the sink. Tripp glanced at him.

Bowen just smiled. "Read it once in a book. The bad guy froze the gems in an ice tray."

Tripp knelt at the bookshelf and inspected the rocks. Same sort of fossils he'd seen at the Willow Hills dig, same sort that decorated Kathy's mantel.

"Know anything about computers, Mac?" Bowen asked. He was sitting in front of Grady's machine toying with the keyboard. The screen was dark. "I don't even know what this is."

"Big," said Tripp. "Never seen this one before, but it looks bigger than a usual PC. Move over." Tripp took Bowen's seat and fiddled with the rear of the panel until the computer came to life. The monitor blinked on and began a quick sequence of changing screens.

"A quick-start or something," said Tripp, more to himself than Bowen, who was watching over his shoulder. "Computer's programmed to do all the start-up procedures by itself automatically. See, watch"—he was pointing to the monitor—"there's sign-on, now a list of utilities. Purely automatic."

The screen had stopped on a cartoon picture of a dinosaur. Over the creature's head the computer had written out: *Good afternoon, Scott. Welcome to the Cenozoic.*

"Smart thing, isn't it," said Bowen, admiringly. "Wonder what it knows about trout?"

"Let's see what's in his files." Tripp entered a series of keystrokes. The screen brought up a long column of initials and dates.

"How'd you learn to do that?" said Bowen, impressed. "Pretty slick."

"Yeah?" said Tripp. "Well, that's about as good as it gets. I can do some basic moves, but this monster's way beyond me. Look"—he pointed at a line of data on the screen—"that entry means, or I think it means, that this is just the outer shell of the filing system. Kind of the tab on a super folder, and the stuff in there goes back through a series of generations."

"Lost me."

"It just means I don't have the slightest idea how to access all this stuff. And there could be a ton of it in here." Tripp entered another series of keystrokes. The screen almost instantly switched to a single column that ended two-thirds of the way down the page. Tripp studied it closely. "Thought it might be something," he said, "but it's not. Sorry."

"Anything at all on there?" asked Bowen, who'd begun fiddling with the phone answering machine.

"Probably," said Tripp. "But it'd take a lot better man than I to find it." He turned the computer off and nodded toward the phone device. "Anything?"

"Listen and learn." Bowen pushed a button.

The machine rewound for fifteen or twenty seconds and then stopped, let off with a kind of mechanical burp, and began playing: "Hi, you've reached the Grady residence.'' Grady's tone was low and measured—and Tripp felt spooked. Bowen's expression was grave. "No one's here to take your call right now, so, at the tone, leave a message and I'll get back to you.''

The voice on the first message was Kathy Sullivan's: "Hi, Scott. Lunch is waiting and so am I. Where are you?'' The tone was friendly, no notes of concern in it, a little exasperated. There followed two more calls from the woman, each growing a little more irritated. Then a new voice. Tripp recognized it immediately.

"It's Monday, Grady. I'm here, you're not. Get your butt in here.'' Carl Crossley. That would have been Monday morning, the opening day of finals, Tripp realized, the day Crossley had to administer 300 tests without Grady. No wonder he was angry. Three more calls from Crossley, all Monday, or so the voice said, all angry.

A new voice on the tape. Tripp recognized it as Howard Donner's: "Scotty, time to talk dissertation. Need to pound out a chapter or two before you head off for the summer. Give me a call.'' Pleasant, no signs of irritation.

Another message, Crossley again: "The Hills starts this week, Grady. If you're not there you are in very serious trouble, young man. Read my lips. You don't show, your career at this school is finished.''

After that, four hang ups as though someone had called and hung up each time after the tape had started. But no messages. Bowen and Tripp looked up at each other across the machine.

"Sure got people riled up,'' observed Bowen.

"Crossley especially," said Tripp. "That was one very ticked off professor."

"The other one, Donner? He sounded okay enough."

Tripp laughed sourly. "Yeah, fellow with an extracurricular activity."

Bowen shot him an uncertain look.

"Tell you over lunch," said Tripp. "Long story."

Silence between the two for a time, both thinking about the tape.

"Downstairs?" said Bowen. Tripp nodded and moved to close the curtain.

"Bowen," he said low over his shoulder, "we got something." His friend came up beside him. Tripp pointed at the sill. The window latch had been wrenched from its socket and was about a half inch out of position. Bare wood marked where it should have sat. The window led out to a fire escape.

"Jimmied," said Bowen.

"Somebody came up the fire escape and popped the window," said Tripp.

"Recent?"

"Can't tell," said Tripp as he moved the window open a few inches and then let it slide closed. "Can't tell when it happened. But you'd expect Grady to fix it if he could, or at least barricade the window if he knew it was broken."

Bowen nodded. "Post-Grady."

"Yeah, post-Grady," agreed Tripp. Someone had broken into the apartment after Grady had disappeared. Just like Kathy's situation, he thought, another break-in. But what were they looking for? "Ideas?"

"Obviously looking for something. Pretty obvious we don't know what."

"Bet that computer knows," said Tripp and silently kicked himself for not knowing more about the machines.

"Or not," said Bowen. "If it did know, wouldn't it make sense for whoever broke in to just take it with him?"

"Maybe he found it and erased it?" offered Tripp. After a bit he added: "Or maybe it was something else in this room that's gone now."

FIFTEEN

A TIRED-LOOKING blue compact was backing out of Wells' driveway as Tripp turned into the street. Tripp slowed and watched as the car pulled up to the next intersection, made a quick U-turn, and headed back toward him. Instinctively Tripp accelerated, pretending he was just another resident hurrying home. He caught a glimpse of a red-haired man as the car flashed past. Tripp waited until the car was well down the street before he made his own lumbering U-turn in the pickup and followed.

With Tripp well behind, the blue car made its way down through the edges of the city toward the university area. After nearly ten minutes of what appeared to be aimless wandering, the car made a slow right onto a street that was all too familiar. Kathy Sullivan's street. Tripp pulled to the curb and watched as the car cruised slowly past Kathy's house, then sped up and disappeared around a far corner. Tripp punched the accelerator on the old truck and was pulling into the next street over before he realized the blue car was on the same street headed his way. The red-haired man looked at him as he passed. Tripp tried again to act casual, like he had business in the neighborhood, but he suspected he had been made. He decided to give the man a little room and headed toward downtown to kill some time.

When Tripp got back to the Rattlesnake, the blue

car was in the driveway. Both front fenders, he could see, were dented in.

Vernon Wells must have been waiting for him. On Tripp's first knock, the door swung open violently to expose a pair of narrow and angry eyes staring at him from across the threshold.

"What do you want?" spat Wells. The voice was nasty and wary.

"Vernon Wells?" asked Tripp.

"What do you want?"

"Few minutes of your time."

"I want to see ID," said Wells, glancing past Tripp at the pickup. "Who are you? Cop?"

"No cop," said Tripp. "Just a guy asking a few questions."

"I saw you following me."

"Wanted to see where you were going."

"Why?"

Enough preliminaries, Tripp decided, wondering if he was looking at a man who had tried to kill him. "Look," he said in a cutting voice, "I know who you are. Now maybe we're going to have a chat about a couple of people, or maybe I just call the police and they come on out and do the chatting for me? *Comprende,* little man?"

Wells seemed to wilt all at once. The angry aggressiveness was replaced by an almost servile passivity. One very strange man, thought Tripp, and he reminded himself to be careful.

"You want to come in?" asked Wells, but he made no move to leave the doorway.

"You know Katherine Sullivan?" Tripp said. It wasn't really a question.

Wells' face colored instantly and his eyes glanced down. "No."

"Wrong answer," said Tripp, lashing the young man with his voice. "Let's talk Kathy Sullivan." Tripp felt himself balling his fists at his side.

"Don't know her," Wells said petulantly.

"Let's cut through the chaff," Tripp hissed. "You've been following her for a couple of years, right? You followed her out here from Boston. Went by her place today. Question is, why?"

"None of your business."

"Look, kid," said Tripp evenly, "it's my business when the woman's a friend of mine."

"There's no law against riding in a car...yet."

"There is if you're stalking a woman." Tripp waited for the kid's reaction. It wasn't long coming. Wells seemed to wilt. His body slumped against the door frame and his head tipped forward, his chin riding down almost to his chest. Tripp shot the words at him: "Why're you following her?"

"She was nice to me," said the young man. "I had some classes with her in Boston and she seemed to care."

"Why'd you come out here?" snapped Tripp.

"I figured she liked me." The voice sounded like a ten-or eleven-year-old talking about a crush. Tripp decided the kid was sicker than he seemed.

"Why'd you go by her house?"

"She's been gone. I've been worried about her."

"How'd you know she's been gone?"

He stammered answering. "I...I sort of keep track of her. I just make sure she's okay. I see her at school and stuff" His voice trailed off.

"You call her?"

"Sometimes."

"But you never talk, right?"

"Just hearing her voice," said Wells, "and I know she's okay."

"Send her mail?"

"Oh!" blurted Wells. It came out like a sob. "It's poetry, you stupid hick farmer."

"But she doesn't want your trash," said Tripp, fighting to control his anger. His words came out in a low gunmetal hiss. "Don't send her any more. *Comprende?*"

A tear rolled down the kid's cheek.

"Why'd you break into her place?"

Wells started as though he'd been slapped. "How'd you know?" he asked, and his voice was small.

"She told me."

"I didn't think she knew. I was careful."

"She didn't know at first," said Tripp. "She was too groggy from the pills. But she figured it out the next day. She's not a stupid woman."

Wells' face had taken on an uncomprehending stare.

"What?" said Tripp.

"What are you talking about?" asked Wells.

"Breaking and entering, creep. Remember?"

"What about pills?" asked Wells.

"What about them?"

"What do they have to do with anything?"

"Pain pills," said Tripp. "Too groggy to realize that some sick creep had broken in and gone through her stuff. You knew she would be."

"I don't know what you're talking about," said Wells. His voice had again taken on a defiant tone.

"I admit I broke into her apartment, but it didn't have anything to do with pills or anything like that. And I didn't take anything. I just wanted…"—he hesitated—"I just wanted to see how she lived."

"You're sick, punk. Woman's lying hurt in the hospital—the hospital you put her in—and you ransack her house." Tripp felt like hitting the kid and had to hold himself back.

"Hospital? What hospital?"

"You're a worm, Wells. She's lying hurt in the hospital and you go through her house. Like a creep."

"You're out of your ignorant mind!" Wells was almost screaming. "You're out of your mind. She was on vacation in Seattle. Not in a hospital."

Tripp snapped to a memory of the picnic conversation. Kathy said she had been on vacation in Seattle during the first break-in—in Boston. Years before.

"Last Monday night?" said Tripp, and for the first time uncertainty was edging into his mind. "You didn't go through her house last Monday night?"

"Last Monday?" whined Wells. "What's last Monday?"

"You didn't start getting obsessed again? Start feeling the same old urges? Trouble, my young friend. Police are gonna want to find out exactly where you were Monday night."

"Stop it!" Wells was openly sobbing. "I admit I went through her place. I told you that. But that was a long time ago. Boston. Not here. I didn't. Not Monday. What hospital?"

"Tell me about Scott Grady," Tripp demanded.

Wells continued to sob, rubbing at his eyes.

"Tell me about Scott Grady," said Tripp, his voice coming back toward a raw and nasty edge.

"He's a friend of hers," Wells managed to say as he tried to control the crying. "That's all I know."

"How good a friend?"

"A friend. That's all I know."

"How do you know?"

A sob heaved across Wells' chest. "I've seen them on campus together. That's all."

"Break into his house, too?"

Wells looked at him vacantly.

"Like you did Sullivan's? Force a window? Go through his stuff?"

"I don't know what you're talking about."

"Grady's house. You broke into it. Why?"

"I don't even know where Grady lives." It was about half sob, half defiant taunt. Like a child.

"Jealous?" said Tripp.

Wells shrugged.

"Hate the guy?" Tripp goaded.

"What's this about?"

"How much do you hate Grady?"

Again the young man shrugged off the question.

"Enough to kill him?"

Wells looked up slowly at Tripp. And began to smile under the watery and reddened eyes. "He's dead?"

"You don't seem too upset."

"I'm not," said Wells, and the smile grew.

"You kill 'im?"

"Hardly." The change in the boy was startling. One minute crying, actually sobbing—the next very much under control, almost seeming to enjoy it. He wondered if the kid was somehow living in a split personality. "Seems like you had plenty of motive," Tripp said levelly.

"Not my kind of crime."

"Sullivan and Grady a coosome twosome? Probably holding hands and touching and doing things lovers do. I'm not surprised you'd kill."

"Save it, farmer," said Wells, his voice steady, his eyes drying. "It's not my type of crime."

"Can you say where you were on the weekend of May 23rd?"

"Probably," responded Wells. "But I'm not going to waste my breath. I don't kill people."

"Police'll ask you."

"And I'll tell them. Not you."

"Not curious how Grady died?" said Tripp, feeling the high ground slipping away.

"Not in the least."

"Where were you last Monday night?"

"Somewhere, probably."

"Why'd you try to kill Kathy Sullivan?"

Wells looked at Tripp for a full ten seconds.

"You're a stupid man," said Vernon Wells. "Now go away." He turned and closed the door firmly. Tripp stood there feeling as if he'd just been sucker-punched by a baby.

TRIPP STOPPED to call Bowen from the same convenience store pay phone he'd used earlier. "Going home," he said to Bowen.

"How'd it go?"

"He's a creep," said Tripp tiredly. "But did he or didn't he? Don't know if I can answer that."

"How'd he seem?"

"Weird. Part of me says he's sick enough to do almost anything. But sick enough to kill? I just don't know."

Tripp walked Bowen through the confrontation.

"Motive," said Bowen, "and maybe opportunity. He's not looking too bad."

"Yeah," agreed Tripp, but he realized that a lot of people were now whirling in the dance. "We've got to find a body. Still on for tomorrow?"

"You bet."

"Ask you another favor?" said Tripp. "I've got a lot of things to chase. Check Donner for me?"

"Where'd he say he was when Grady apparently departed this earthly orb?"

"Forest service meeting in Idaho," said Tripp. "The Red Lion in Coeur d'Alene. Said he was there from Wednesday through Saturday. Also see if he's leaving town."

"I'll check it."

"How's Kathy?"

"Depressed, I think. She's in her room. Wants to go home."

"You've got to keep her there."

"I'll try."

One more call. Tripp had begun to wonder if maybe he shouldn't get a phone, for at least a while.

Helen Crossley answered almost at once. Tripp explained his search for Scott Grady. She said she was doubtful she could help but would see Tripp the next morning.

It was growing dark by the time Tripp made it back to the cabin. The Bells were impatient for their food, and the pines across the meadow were hidden in a chilly mist. Keeping a cautious eye on the shadows, Tripp fed the horses, then built himself a drink and walked out to the wood shop. The acrid smell of smoke and charred wood still hung in the air. Tripp kicked at the ashes where he'd doused the fire. The flames had crawled up the wall but had done little damage beyond charring the wood. One end of a work table showed the blackened remains of a tongue of fire, but overall the shop was in remarkably good shape.

The small boat sat unharmed beneath the ash-covered tarp. Tripp pulled the canvas back and the boat gleamed under the lights, its unfinished form beckoning him like an old friend who wanted to talk. He wiped dust from the sides and ran his finger along the seam of caulk that joined wood and Plexiglas. He rigged a block with sandpaper and began stroking the teak railing, but his mind was on Kathy Sullivan.

He pictured her at Bowen's, her arm in a sling, the wisp of hair hanging in her face. He chewed back and forth on the events of the past few days. Grady gone—dead, probably. Donner—did he have a motive to kill? Maybe not. Wells—maybe in his sick frustration enough anger and hatred to kill. Hunt—nothing obvious. Crossley—nothing obvious, but lingering scents that not all was as it appeared. Helen Crossley—an empty page. Corry Sound—another empty page. Pages that needed to be filled, dots that needed to be found and connected. And Kathy Sullivan—not even in his universe a week ago. Now the center.

SIXTEEN

B<small>Y</small> M<small>ONAY</small> <small>MORNING</small> the skies had cleared and the air was warm and crystalline. The peaceful chatter of lawn sprinklers and the smell of freshly mowed grass marked Tripp's route through the college neighborhood to the Crossley house.

Helen Crossley answered the door dressed to the nines, a low-cut black silk blouse showing more than a hint of décolletage, a large red leather belt cinched tightly around her narrow waist. Below that a pair of form-fitting black tights left little to the imagination. Tripp judged her to be in her mid-forties—younger than her husband—and well preserved in an artificial sort of way. Money had unobviously been spent on her eyes and chin, and her smile dazzled against straight white teeth.

"Oh, the famed Mr. Tripp," she cooed as she answered the door and showed him inside. "Whole campus is just buzzing, you know, that a private eye is snooping around. Just buzzing. What a treat. This way." She led him into the kitchen. "I bet a man like you takes his coffee black."

Tripp merely nodded, suspecting Helen Crossley had read more than her share of whodunits. It was already beginning to have the markings of a long day.

"Of course, black," she said. "I knew it." Handing him a cup, she directed Tripp through sliding doors to a patio where she arranged them at a circular table. "I just so adore the morning sun out here," she said. "Don't you?" Tripp said he did.

Helen Crossley made a production of tasting her coffee and fishing a cigarette from a hand-tooled leather case. She handed Tripp the lighter and managed to give him an ample glimpse of chest as she bent to the flame. "So," she gushed, breathing out a trail of blue smoke, "a private investigator. Where do we begin?"

"Well," said Tripp, "this isn't really an investigation."

Helen Crossley looked confused.

"What I mean to say," he added quickly, "is that I'm not actually a licensed investigator. But I am looking into the Grady case." Helen brightened considerably.

"I have so adored that boy," she said. "Tragedy, really."

"Tragedy, Mrs. Crossley?"

"Tragedy certainly, Ben. May I call you Ben? Tragedy that a boy like that would just up and chuck it all. With such a promising future ahead. Tragedy." Another long breath of smoke. She actually looked on the verge of tears. Tripp suspected Helen Crossley had been a college drama major a long time before.

"Do you know him well?" asked Tripp.

"Oh my." She sighed. "He was like a son to us."

"Was?" asked Tripp.

The woman seemed momentarily at a loss for words. "I mean is, certainly. We both so adore him."

Tripp thought about Donner's portrait of the

Crossleys as cannibals, licking their lips at the thought of Grady. He found himself staring at her teeth. "So you spent a lot of time with Scott?"

"Well, Carly certainly did," she said. "The dig up north. Summers there every year. And of course the time at school. Scott was—is—Carly's teaching assistant, you know."

"Had Grady's work slowed down this year?"

The look of confusion again as she stubbed out her cigarette. "Hardly, Ben." She seemed to enjoy correcting him. "If anything, they were working even harder. Even in the evenings around here, Carly was forever on the phone trying to find Scott or arranging for a meeting."

Tripp kept his face neutral, though Helen's words didn't fit with her husband's. "You know what they might have been working on?"

"Bones, bones, bones." She laughed. "What else is there in life?"

"I mean specifically?"

"Bones are as specific as I get, Ben. I made a conscious decision a long time ago that I wouldn't become involved in Carly's work. It's much too"—she seemed to be searching for a word—"it's much too scientific. Bones are as deep as I go." She laughed and looked at Tripp for approval.

He smiled. "Mrs. Crossley, we think Scott disappeared the weekend of May 23rd, 24th. The 23rd, actually. That was a Saturday and I wonder—"

She interrupted him. "Oh my," she said, brightening, "you're looking for an alibi for me, aren't you?" She seemed elated. "Just like in all the books?"

"Just trying to put things together," said Tripp lightly. "So I can rule you out, you understand."

"Oh, perfectly, perfectly." Helen Crossley was almost purring, and Tripp imagined the mileage she'd get out of it with her friends.

"Saturday, May 23rd?" prompted Tripp.

"Well, let's see." More drama coaching, thought Tripp. "Let me think—so many little things rattling around in this head of mine. The 23rd? A Saturday? Well, now, that's an easy one. Now, the week before I threw the faculty tea for the whole department. Thirteen wives and assorted hangers-on. My, what an experience, let me tell you." She was gushing again. Tripp was beginning to appreciate Crossley's choice of a tent two months out of the year. Though he didn't quite believe Helen Crossley was as dizzy as she let on.

"I simply adore most of those women. But there are some real vipers, let me tell you. But, yes"— she looked around blankly, momentarily confused—"oh yes, now the 23rd. The tea was the 16th. Saturday the 16th, and it just exhausted me. You've no idea. I thought I was having a nervous breakdown. So I made, absolutely made Carly take me away. Such a dear, such a dear. He took me shopping in Seattle the very next weekend. That'd be the 23rd, wouldn't it? Saturday and Sunday. A marvelous trip. I think I would have just died if he hadn't taken me away."

"Seattle?" said Tripp.

"Oh my, yes," she said. "We do that as often as we can. Nordstrom, The Bon, Frederick's...stores you just can't find in this part of the world. And it's only an hour away."

"You fly?" asked Tripp. He hadn't thought about flying anywhere in years.

"It's just an hour," said Helen. "Lovely service in first. Though it's gone downhill since just everyone started flying." She looked sad. But she brightened. Tripp had the uncanny feeling he was watching a local TV anchor bunny exuding all the facial gestures appropriate to her stories—happy, sad, happy, concerned. "Carly came home exhausted from the office Friday, and we just sort of hopped off to Seattle. The very next morning. God, I would have died if I'd not gotten some time off."

"So you left Saturday?"

"Saturday morning. Glorious Saturday morning."

Saturday—the day Grady disappeared—Crossley was in Seattle. Tripp needed to check the airlines.

"And just one more thing, Mrs. Crossley?" he said. "An auto wreck a week or so ago might somehow be connected with this case and..."

"Anyone we know?" she asked. Concern again.

"Another professor from the university."

Helen Crossley made a face of deep sadness.

"Nothing major, though," said Tripp. "But I wonder—again just by way of ruling things out—mind if I take a look at your car?"

The woman seemed almost overjoyed. "You want to see my car? Oh, delicious. I understand completely. How I adore crime things like this. Please, Ben, follow me."

Her high-heeled pumps tapping on the tiles, Helen Crossley led Tripp back through the kitchen past a laundry room into a two car garage. A small Mercedes coupe sat against the far wall.

"Carly gave it to me for my twenty-ninth birthday...last year," she said coquettishly, giggling. "Isn't it adorable? Here, inspect it, inspector," and she led him around the car. It was pristine.

"Where's your husband's car?"

"Oh, that old beast of a thing?" said the woman, wrinkling her face in disgust. "Probably in some mud hole up in Canada, I would expect."

"He drives it to the dig?"

"Why wouldn't he? It's his whole little world on wheels. Rocks and hammers and all that stuff in the back. Carly and his car are almost one and the same. Kind of dusty and filled with rocks." She laughed, and Tripp suspected the Crossley honeymoon had long since ended.

The woman held his arm as Tripp walked back to the pickup.

"Where now, inspector?"

"Oh," said Tripp, "more people, more talk."

"You have any suspects?" she whispered melodramatically.

"Just you, Mrs. Crossley," he whispered back.

She seemed momentarily stunned and then burst out laughing. "Oh my, I adore that. Tough and cynical man. It's just like the books."

"Sure is," Tripp said.

"Any time you're in the neighborhood, just drop in. Do. So much fun." She arched her eyebrows flirtatiously as she offered her hand in farewell. "I'd adore seeing you again."

Tripp pulled away from the curb trying to figure whether he'd just been conned—or propositioned.

BOWDEN'S new green Jeep was in the university parking lot as Tripp arrived for their search of the office.

"How went the tryst with our Mrs. Crossley, Juan?" he asked as they fell into step toward the sciences building.

Tripp shot a questioning glance from the corner of his eye. "You knew something about her I didn't?"

Bowen laughed. "University wife? Alone all the time? Married to a professor? And along comes Mr. Studly? Figured it might get steamy."

"Odd one," said Tripp. "Not my type. Couple of things to check out, though. One, Crossley's car isn't here."

"Not all that unusual," observed Bowen. "Wouldn't you expect him to take it with him to Shelby?"

"I suppose," said Tripp. "But John Hunt said Crossley drives around most of the time in a state car. Odd. I could kick myself for not looking for it when I was up there. But he's alibied: He and his wife went to Seattle the weekend Grady disappeared. Anything on our good Professor Donner?"

"Got reservations for London all right. But the other part doesn't completely check out," said Bowen. Tripp offered his friend another sideways glance as they walked across a grass-covered square.

"He was in Coeur d'Alene all right," said Bowen. "I got the hotel manager to go through the books. At least the books say he was there. Along with about a dozen other people there for the meeting. But he checked out on Friday, not Saturday."

"Friday?" said Tripp. "Then he wasn't there through Saturday as he said?"

"Would appear thus," said Bowen. "Manager double-checked with the guy who was on the desk. Guy remembered Donner well. Said Donner had reservations to Saturday and paid his bill to Saturday. But he checked out Friday afternoon sometime. Desk guy can't remember exactly when, probably late in the day. But it was Friday when he left."

"So," said Tripp, "our strange Mr. Donner was a couple hundred miles away in Idaho on Friday the 22nd. But he could have been anywhere by Saturday." Tripp ran the Donner meeting over in his mind. He had said he was in Idaho on Saturday. "He didn't tell us the truth."

"Your mind's an incredible thing."

"Odd that he'd lie about it," said Tripp. "Day Grady disappears, and Donner's lying about where he was."

"Probably a highway diner," offered Bowen.

The teenager of the week before was gone from the reception desk. In her place was an efficient young man who let them into Grady's vacant office with little fuss or ceremony.

The office turned out to be no more than an enclosed, windowless cubicle—a metal desk, filing cabinet, and chair filling its crowded space. Metal bookshelves crammed with papers and texts hung from three walls, and cardboard cartons overflowing with large chunks of rock and fossilized bone spilled against the baseboards.

"Where to start?" Bowen sighed as the two men squeezed inside.

Tripp sat down at the desk. "I'll do this, you take the files."

"And remind me again what we're looking for?" said Bowen.

"A body. So start with the Bs."

Tripp opened the top drawer of the desk. It proved to be much like its cousin in Grady's apartment, filled with chips of rock and bone, a jeweler's loupe, pencil stubs, and the other odd detritus of a scientist's nest.

"Phew," said Bowen, paging through a foot-thick stack of papers. "This guy really worked for a living. There must be dozens of reports and papers in here. Not all his, but a lot of 'em are. Listen to the name of this one"—he pulled a thick report from amid the other papers—" 'The Effect on Vocalization of IntraSpecial Soft Palate Mutation in the Upper Jurassic.' That mean it's about talking dinosaurs?"

"So Mr. Ed wasn't an original concept, huh?" said Tripp without turning. "What're the dates?"

Bowen scanned over the reports. "All last year."

"Keep your eyes peeled for anything from this year."

Tripp found a pile of what appeared to be similar papers in another drawer and paged slowly through them. Most were from the year before, even the year before that. Not much current. The bottom drawer held more reports and a thick file of what appeared to be master sheets for tests.

Bowen had begun sorting through the bookshelves. The first rack proved to be almost all published literature from other scientists. A second shelf was mostly textbooks and reference works. "If there's something in here," he said finally, "I'm too stupid to recognize it."

"I had the same thought," said Tripp. He began on another wall of shelves. "What's bothering me is that there's nothing so far to indicate what he'd been working so hard on this year, if he was. Most everything's from the year before or even earlier."

Bowen nodded as he pulled out another book. "You're right. If he was working that hard this year, where's the work?"

"And also," said Tripp, "where're all the notes he must have been leaving when he went climbing? Seen anything like that yet?"

Bowen shrugged. "Maybe he tossed 'em."

Tripp started on the boxes along the floor. Large fossil bones poked out from the top of the first carton. Tripp sorted around among the rocks but found only more. The second was closed. Inside, more rocks, an old pair of sneakers, more rocks. Another open box and more bones. Another closed. Tripp removed the lid. Filled with papers.

"Bingo," said Tripp. "Climb notes."

"Lord," said Bowen, "look at the size of that stack!" Tripp had pulled out a nearly inch-thick pile of papers. "All climbs?" Bowen asked as Tripp paged quickly through them.

"And bingo again, maybe," said Tripp, bending into the open carton and lifting out a string-tied bundle of small colored notebooks. "Field books, a scientist's best friend," he said, recalling Crossley thumbing through his notebook at Willow Hills. "They write down everything—and I mean everything—bones to bowel movements. If it's here," he said, waving the bundle, "it's here."

Bowen looked around the small room. "Think we could purloin these documents? Gettin' awfully sick of this little cell. Stuff might go down better over a nice tall drink."

"Well, *if* there had been a crime, I suppose the police would have impounded this stuff *if* they had thought to look here," said Tripp. "But we don't have a crime yet, eh? I'll distract the young pepster down at the desk."

"Meet you on the back porch," said Bowen to Tripp's receding back.

"ISN'T IT against the law to take this stuff?" Kathy asked, surveying the papers and notebooks heaped on the porch's wooden table next to a pitcher of iced tea and three tall glasses.

"Not if we're not caught," said Bowen.

Kathy hefted the stack of climbing notes. "Lot of stuff here." She paged through the notes. "Feels spooky."

"It is," said Tripp.

"Climbing notes, latest on top," she said. "Shall I read?" The men nodded.

"'May 16,'" she began and looked up. Tripp was making notes on a yellow legal pad. "That was just a week before he vanished," said Kathy. "God, this is weird. 'May 16. Bitterroots. Roundover escarpment, south face, Gulley's Ridge. Up and back.'" She looked up. "Any of this make sense?"

Tripp looked at his notes. "I'd guess it means some sort of climb in the Bitterroot Mountains south of here," he said. "Climbers would know. The rest is probably the exact route: south face of the Roundover cliff or escarpment along Gulley's

Ridge. I'm assuming that's an ascent. 'Up and back' I suppose means up and back the same day. Nothing later than May 16? Closer to when he disappeared? Anything from the 22nd or 23rd?''

Kathy paged through the top several sheets and shook her head. ''Everything's older,'' she said. ''Want me to read more?'' Tripp nodded. Bowen sipped his tea.

''Next one,'' she said. '''May 2nd, 3rd. Bitterroots, Little Chief, west face, Crawler's Pinnacle, 11,000 feet. Midway RON.''' She looked up again.

''Midway R-O-N,'' said Tripp. ''Think R-O-N means remainder of night. Midway, I suppose, is midway up the climb. Climbed Little Chief down in the Bitterroots, stayed in a tent overnight, and came down the next day. Next?''

'''April 18th. The Garnets, Teepee Peak, south buttress, Widow's Walk: 11,200 to 12,400. Up and back.'''

''The next sheet April 5th?'' Tripp asked.

''April 5th,'' said Kathy, looking up at Tripp. ''How'd you know?''

Tripp shrugged and read from his own notes. ''May 16th, May 2nd, April 18th. Looks like he climbed about every two weeks. Sound right?''

''I thought he climbed all the time,'' said Kathy. ''I mean, most weekends it was tough to even get in touch with him. He'd be off on some rock somewhere.''

Tripp nodded her back toward the stack.

''Next one,'' said Kathy, ''the next one is from March 14th. 'March 14. Ice climb. Bitterroots, Twin Angels, south peak, Crystal Falls, 9,300. Up and back.'''

Kathy sorted through the sheets and looked up. "March 14th to April 4th is three weeks. Scott never went three weeks between climbs. It was like a religion to him. He was up there almost every weekend."

"Maybe he was climbing but just didn't always leave a note?" suggested Bowen.

"No, that was his other religion," said Kathy. "He always left a note." She lit a cigarette. No argument.

"Why don't you slip back a year or so," suggested Tripp. "See if the two-week pattern holds."

Kathy paged back to the center of the stack of notes.

"A year earlier okay?" she asked. "'June 1, Trapper Peak, south buttress, Widow's Walk, 11,500 to 13,000. Up and back.' I guess he likes that climb."

Tripp noticed Kathy was still referring to Grady in the present tense. He doubted it was accurate.

She sorted through more papers. "Okay, here's the weekly pattern that I was telling you about," she said. "Climb before Trapper Peak June 1st a year ago is May 24th. Let's see…climb before that is May 17th. Next one"—she turned back one page—"next one's May 16th. That's more like what I know: every week, sometimes twice a week."

"Okay," said Tripp. "That's at least suspicious. A year ago he's climbing twice a week. Now a year later he's climbing only once every two or three weeks. We need to go through the dates one by one and figure out exactly when the change in pattern occurred." Tripp suspected they'd find it was right around Christmas when—apparently—everything about Scott Grady changed.

Kathy picked up the climb notes and started reading dates. Through the first three months of the year, Grady was climbing about every two weeks.

"Okay," she said, "here's where the pattern breaks. The climb before December 21st was December 15th. Then the day before, the 14th. Next entry is December 7th. Next, December 1st." She looked back through the stack. "All the climbs in early December are a week or less apart. After the 21st, they start to get further and further apart, usually two weeks."

Tripp scanned his notes. "So he was climbing regularly up until the last week in December. And then it became sporadic. What was the December 21st climb?"

Kathy looked through the notes. "'December 21st. Ice climb, south Bitterroots, Soldiers' Knoll, the Caterpillar: 6,800. RON Darby.'"

"Another climb in the Bitterroots," said Tripp, scanning down the line of dates he'd written on the legal pad. "Up until late December last year, Grady was climbing every weekend, sometimes a couple of times each weekend. Then something happens around December 21st, right before Christmas. The pattern changes. The frequency of his climbs is cut in half. So what happened on December 21st, or right after?" Tripp looked around the table at his friends. Bowen had picked up the climb notes and was paging through them. Kathy was looking back at Tripp, her eyes firm, determined.

"He was still climbing, Ben," she said. "There

may not be any notes to prove it, but he was still climbing. He told me.''

Tripp nodded. "Okay," he said, "he was still climbing. So the climb notes are either missing or he didn't leave any. Let's see what the field notes say." He took the top notebook from the stack and began paging through.

"And?" said Bowen.

"Well, it's not current," said Tripp. "The last entry is April 30th, this year."

"Each book is a month's worth?" asked Bowen.

Tripp flipped through the small book. "Monthly," he said. "First entry is Wednesday, April 1st. Last entry—Thursday, April 30th."

"No book for May?" asked Kathy. Tripp opened the two dozen books one at a time and scanned the dates. "No book for May this year," he said finally.

"Probably had it with him," offered Bowen.

Tripp was back in the April field book. "Some strange entries here. Or maybe they're not strange to a paleontologist. Listen to this: 'Thursday, April 30. Grade tests a.m. Review finals late a.m. J p.m. to a.m.'"

"What's a J?" said Bowen.

"Big J," said Tripp, "all alone. J." He passed the book along to Bowen. Kathy leaned over to look.

"Jejune," offered Bowen, handing it back.

"Another," said Tripp. "'Wednesday, April 29. Frosh test late a.m. J p.m. to late.' Ideas, anybody?" Tripp looked around the table.

"Is J on every page?" said Bowen.

Tripp scanned back through the notebook. "Almost," he said. "Looks like he did the other stuff he needed to do early in the morning or at least until noon and then started on J, whatever it is.''

Tripp carefully paged back through eight field books, comparing them with the homemade calendar he'd roughed out on his pad. At length he set them down and took a long sip of his own drink, looking at Kathy.

"Weekends when you thought he was climbing he's listed J, whatever it is," said Tripp. "And it's J all the way back to two days after Christmas. The first J entry is December 27th. Nothing...no Js before that."

A long silence around the table.

"So," said Bowen, finally. "J. A who or maybe a what."

Tripp nodded. "A who or a what that came to consume one very large portion of Scott Grady's time. Mean anything at all to either of you?"

"I've never heard it before in my life," Kathy said quietly. "It's spooky."

"Maybe J means some kind of work," said Bowen. "Jigsawing, or jogging, maybe."

Kathy: "He doesn't jog."

"Just joshing," said Bowen.

"Couple of things here," Tripp said finally. "Everyone has talked about a change in Grady beginning early this year. Think it'd be fair to say it's connected with J, whatever that is. The Js start happening right at the time his work pattern starts to change, and also right at the time he starts changing the frequency of his climbs. Think we've got to assume they're connected.

"What we've got," Tripp continued slowly, almost to himself, "what we've got is a pattern.

Grady changes a lot in December, according to everyone around him. At the same time he begins to slack off on his climbing, or at least in writing down his climbs. Same time we get the first use of the J thing in his notes. So J and the changes must be tied.''

"But what—or who," interrupted Bowen, "is J?"

All three sipped their drinks.

"Okay then," said Tripp. "We start over. Go back and start asking people what J means."

"Who do you start with?" said Kathy.

"The Js," said Tripp simply.

"How 'bout if I take the Ws?" offered Bowen. "As in Wells?"

"I don't think so," said Kathy, uncertainly.

"We've got to talk to him again," said Tripp. "And there's Donner and Crossley, Helen Crossley, too. John Hunt. Corry Sound."

They were quiet for a while. The light had fallen and they were in near darkness on the porch.

"I'll look for Corry Sound tomorrow," said Tripp.

"A grand idea, lad," said Bowen. "And I'll have a solemn visitation with our young poet Mr. Wells. Love to show him the rapier edge of a truly keen intellect."

"I need to go home, Ben," said Kathy. Her face was in shadow, but Tripp could hear the tiredness in her voice.

"I know it's tough," said Tripp, "but you have to give it another day." He thought to himself again that whatever had driven someone to try to kill them once was most definitely still out there. They still weren't safe, wouldn't be until they had gotten to the root of Grady's disappearance. "One more day."

"You're a broken record."

"I don't want to be a dead record," said Tripp. "And I don't want you to be one either."

SEVENTEEN

TRIPP CHECKED IN first thing the next morning at the Rock Creek ranger station. They told him a mapper from the survey was working at the end of the road, some twenty miles up. He turned his truck up the canyon.

The dirt road followed an easy grade up through the wild country, spectacular scenery crowding in on either side. In some areas it widened out and Tripp could make out the high, notched peaks of the Bitterroots well to the west. Most of the way, though, was narrow canyon, the waters of Rock Creek eddying along through boulders and deadfalls, in some places cutting right to the edge of the road, in others lost beyond willow and tamarack meadows.

Just beyond twenty miles the road suddenly ended. No signs, no warnings. A couple of granite boulders marking a final terminus. Tripp killed the engine and got out.

Around him, the deceptive stillness of high mountains. At first his ears could make out nothing. A deep, abiding quiet. Then slowly, almost imperceptively, the sounds began to register, as though his brain was somehow stripping away filters it had built up to ward off the noises of urban life...and beginning to hear.

First, a bird—maybe a hawk. High and far away: a shrill-pitched, almost reddish sound, a quick shriek into the stillness. Then insects. Flies and bees droning, a soft yellow liquid sound that seemed to fill up all the cracks of quiet. Then the faint bluish rush of trees catching and turning small breezes in their boughs.

Suddenly, off to the east, the stillness was broken by the explosive detonation of a big engine grinding to life. It roared across the quiet like some angry pistoned monster—a Caterpillar tractor firing up, its concussive reports echoing back and forth across the canyon. Tripp craned to see, but the source was above and beyond the green wall of pine fronting the road. The bees and the hawk and the trees were buried in its noise.

Tripp backed the pickup down the road until he came to a rough logging trail cut into the canyon wall. He turned and followed it up for nearly a mile before it leveled off. In the distance a wide area of forest had been cleared, all the great pine trunks severed at ground level as though by some giant scythe. Beyond in the rough, chewed-up landscape, the Caterpillar he had heard from below was pushing dead brush into an enormous pile.

Tripp pulled the truck up to the Cat. A big man with a full beard and a huge pot belly waved from the open seat. Sunlight reflected dully from his worn metal hard hat. Bib overalls covered stained long-sleeved underwear. The operator pushed a lever and the engine died to silence.

"Morning," said Tripp. "Maybe you can help me. Looking for a woman."

The wide face under the graying whiskers broke into a broad grin. "Sure are looking in the wrong spot, buster." Laughter rolled across his broad belly. The man turned to the other side and spat in the dirt. "This a logging camp, mister. Not some singles bar." More mirth in the girth, and Tripp willed himself to be patient.

"Trying to find a woman up here doing some mapping for the government. Ranger station said she's up in these parts."

Another spit to the side. "Well, now..."

Suddenly a violent sharp clang as a bullet careened off metal. Tripp instinctively dove for the ground, the big man tumbling from the tractor not far behind him. Another shot—this time Tripp actually heard the rifle—and another ricochet off the Cat. Sounded too much like Vietnam. Tripp tried to bury his head in the dirt, wondering in rising fear if somehow Grady's killer had followed him. Maybe the same shadow that had stalked him to the cabin. He realized he wasn't armed, couldn't shoot back. Felt helpless. Beside him the big man sat up...and started laughing.

"Okay," the man bellowed, "you no good sidewinder sow belly, knock it off!" His voice echoed around the mountainside. Answered by another rifle shot and they both ducked. "Enough now, boy!" the man roared. "Can't you see we got company down here?"

No more shots. The big man stood up and dusted off his filthy overalls. Offered Tripp a hand up. Tripp rose uncertainly, looking about him for the shooter.

"My half-wit brother," offered the man. "Stupid hen's idea of fun." He chuckled gleefully. A man with a rifle cradled in his arms emerged from the tree line. The big man waved. "We got company here!" he shouted. The rifleman waved back.

The big man turned and clumsily tried to brush the dirt from Tripp's shirt. "Sorry," he said in a good-natured way. "Brother's idea of entertainment."

The other man walked up. As large as the Cat driver was, his brother was small. Thin, raw boned. Cheeks burned salmon red. Adam's apple prominent in a turkey neck.

"Get over here and apologize," said the big man, grabbing the smaller one by the shoulder. He pushed the man toward Tripp. Both brothers were grinning self-consciously.

"Sorry," said the small one. "I'm a good shot, though. Wouldn't get ya." The brothers laughed. The big one sized Tripp up.

"You local?"

"Local," said Tripp, trying to calm down the sudden case of shakes invading his hands. "Like I was saying, up here looking for a woman mapping in these parts. Seen anything like that?" He jammed his hands into his pockets.

"Yeah, she's up here," offered the large brother.

"You've seen her?"

"Her and that hyena dog of hers," said the scrawny one.

"Think it's a wolf," offered the big one. "But yeah, she's up here. And I'll warn you, mister, she's a hard case. Don't think I'd get near without a pretty big gun." They both chuckled uncomfortably.

"You got troubles with her?"

"Don't have no business up here," sneered the little brother. Big brother made to shush him.

"Brother here was running on about half his cyl-inders," said the bigger man. "Decided to have a little fun with the woman. She didn't think his target practice was funny. Sicced that dog on him." Big brother chortled. Little brother turned away. "But we're friendly now," he added, waving his hand off toward the slope above them. "She stays up there, we stay down here. Friends. Right, half amp?" He laughed.

"Where's there?" asked Tripp.

"Road at the tree line," said the big man, point-ing. "Follow it up about couple of miles. Branches off here and there, but stay on the main trail. She's got a camp couple miles up."

Tripp turned to go.

"Be sure to give her our regards," said the big man, and laughter rolled across his belly.

Tripp found the road—actually more of a path—and pushed his pickup into the forest. Pine boughs scraped along his doors like fingernails on black-boards as the old truck lunged back and forth from one bear grass clump to another.

In compound low, he was nearly twenty minutes driving before the wall of pines gave way to a small clearing. A well-used World War II-vintage Jeep sat against a lean-to formed of skinny lodgepole roofed over with a bright yellow plastic tarp. Under it, a handful of plastic storage crates, a few jugs, and some black garbage bags filled and tied off. Nearby, a small red Alpine tent, its nylon door zipped closed. A canvas-webbed director's chair sat in front of the tent. In the center of it all, a campfire pit ringed by heavy rocks.

Tripp unzipped the tent flap and glanced inside:

a sleeping bag and a Coleman lantern, a light back-pack. He closed the flap and poked through the gear under the lean-to. The jugs contained some sort of acid, an acrid smell that burned the eyes. Two storage boxes held food: canned foods in one, boxed dehydrated meals in the other. A third storage bin held papers: maps mostly—some of them rudimentary sketches, others full-color glossies—and notes about maps. Yet another box held photos bundled in plastic Baggies. Tripp held them up: They were obviously photos of mountains, but they seemed somehow blurred. Tripp tried focusing and unfocusing his eyes, but the photos would not come into resolution. Digging down through the Baggies, he came on a small wooden box. Stereoscopic Viewer, said the label. He was trying to load a photo into the device when a soft growl floated across the camp from behind him. The hairs on the back of his neck stood straight up. He turned carefully toward the sound.

Across the clearing, just under the trees, a woman and a dog. The black-and-white dog was standing rigidly still, its eyes on his eyes, its lips curled back to show teeth. Another soft growl. Tripp felt himself pushing his hands into the air like a crook surrendering to police. The woman stood equally still, watching him. Medium height, blond hair mostly hidden under a baseball cap, dusty blue jeans, a khaki vest—her mouth tight and serious.

Tripp smiled nervously. "Howdy," he said. It sounded lame. "You Corry Sound?" The dog growled again.

The woman's voice was cautious, controlled. "Who are you?"

"Name's Ben Tripp. Howard Donner at the university told me how to find you."

The woman seemed to relax a little. The dog didn't. "Donner tell you to look through my stuff?"

Tripp glanced sideways at the opened storage box. "Sorry, but I was bored. A little curious. You really are mapping up here, huh?" Tripp let his hands ease down, and the dog noted it with another soft snarl.

"I'm Corry. You're who again?"

"Ben Tripp. I'm investigating the disappearance of a guy you know. Scott Grady?"

A look of confusion swept across her face. "Blue, sit." The dog immediately sat, but it never took its eyes off Tripp. The woman entered the clearing. The dog remained behind.

Tripp gestured behind him. "Loggers back there directed me."

"Nice Montana gentlemen," said the woman.

"Thoroughbreds," agreed Tripp.

"You said you're here about Scott. What about Scott?"

"You haven't heard?"

"Heard what?"

"Been missing for more than a month."

"I hadn't heard," she said, concern in her voice, her eyes probing Tripp, who still stood awkwardly near the lean-to. She called her dog over and told it to lie down. It obeyed automatically. "Relax," she said to Tripp and settled onto the director's chair, uncapping a canteen from her belt and taking a long drink. She offered it to Tripp. He shook his head.

"Tell me about Scott," said Corry. "Missing?"

Tripp found himself repeating the now-familiar story of Grady's disappearance during finals, his own conversations with people who knew Grady. "Your name came up quite a bit," said Tripp. "You worked with Scott last year?"

Corry nodded.

"But you hadn't heard of his disappearance?"

She shook her head. "I've been up here since the snows cleared. Maybe a couple of trips to town for supplies. Couple of trips to the survey office. But I hadn't heard."

"Last time you saw Scott?"

The woman seemed to search through her mind. "Probably end of April. Right about then."

"Where?"

"School," she said. "I saw him in the hall. Chatted. But it was brief, nothing much. Casual." She was quiet for a time. "Yeah, I suppose it was the end of April. I came up here first week in May. So that'd be about right."

Tripp thought back through the reported changes in Grady's work habits. "Had you seen much of him before that?"

The woman shook her head. "Hallway encounters mostly, I suppose. I wasn't really spending much time at school. I'd be up there once in awhile and maybe run into him."

Tripp recalled his visit with Donner—and the professor's description of her as bright—and real. Obviously bright, he thought to himself, and eyes that were open and honest. "One person I talked to said you and Scott had been close last year?"

Corry leaned over and patted the dog's head. It still hadn't stopped watching Tripp. She took her time answering. "We worked together," she said carefully, "but that was awhile back."

"Year ago? Year and a half ago?"

She nodded. "Year ago. Why the question?"

They both turned to the low roar of the Caterpillar firing into life again down the mountain.

"God, I hate those people," she said.

Tripp looked at her questioningly.

"They destroy everything. New growth, old growth. They clear cut, knock everything down. Rip off the covering brush. Watercourses change, erosional patterns shift, whole habitats disappear. Animals starve to death because of them."

"You asked why," said Tripp. "The why of it is, I'm pounding around in the dark on this thing right now. Grady's gone—I suspect he's dead—and somebody out there knows the why and the how. I'm trying to put enough pieces of this puzzle together to find out who that is. So the why is…the why is I've got to find all the pieces."

"You suspect he's dead?" Her clear blue eyes boring into his.

"He's been gone more than a month now. Searched his apartment. He hadn't packed for a trip. Mail unanswered. Couple of other strange things happening. Yeah. I think he's dead. And I'm trying to put it together."

"Well, I don't know if I'm a piece of that," she said. "We worked pretty intensely on a project for six months. Then we didn't. I mean, the project was over and we both went our separate ways."

"Were you and Scott romantically involved?"

Tripp was surprised to hear the woman laugh.

"Donner say that?" she asked. "That'd be something Donner would say."

"Actually no. I'm just wondering."

"Sorry, but that's Donner. Or that scum Crossley." Her laughter faded. "No, we weren't romantic. Just friends. No boy-girl thing. It's astounding, though, how those professors get their rocks off."

"You called Crossley scum?"

"A polite term." She smiled. "For mixed company."

"My turn to ask why."

"Simply because he is," she said. She gestured at the camp around her. "Like my summer condo here? Nice soft bed with pressed linens? Great view out the balcony." She snorted out a derisive chuckle. "All courtesy Carl Crossley."

Tripp kept quiet as she rose from her seat and rummaged through the storage box with the maps. Producing a wad an inch thick, she dropped it in Tripp's lap and returned to her chair.

"That's what I do now. Take a look at them."

Tripp flipped through the sheets.

"Maps," she said. "Geologic maps. I trudge around up here in the back of nowhere and build maps of what the geology is. Ophiolitic sequences, xenoliths, sheeted diabases, exotic terranes, dikes, plugs." She shook her head in disgust, seemed to recollect herself, looked up smiling. But it was a smile without humor, without pleasure. "And I do it because of Carl Crossley."

"Scum, you say?"

"Because he's made sure I can't do anything else right now." Absently she leaned down and scratched her dog behind the ear. When she spoke, her tones were measured and concise. "For a year now, Crossley's blocked my dissertation. I would have had my doctorate, been out working, doing something useful—maybe even teaching." She made a wry face at the word. "But Crossley's blocked everything."

Tripp recalled Crossley's description of Sound as unorganized, unfocused…afraid to go out in the world. This didn't seem like the same person.

"How's he blocking your dissertation?"

"Just won't approve it. Finds this and that to criticize. Doesn't like the overall concept. One thing, then another, and I've been pretty much on hold for a year or more. That's why I'm doing this." She spread out her arms and gestured around the camp. "Only thing I'm qualified for. Mapping. No doctorate, no good job. Just killing time. Trying to get into another school."

"Another school?"

"I'm stalled here. Crossley's not gonna let me get through. So I'm trying to transfer everything to another school. Means starting over, pretty much, but it's worth it."

"Why's he doing it?"

"If I knew, I could fix it. But I don't so I can't."

"Think it's your work?"

She snorted out a laugh and her blue eyes were crystal hard. "Hardly. I know what's out there and my stuff is good. Better than good. My stuff's excellent. Maybe it's because I won't get involved with him."

Tripp looked at her quizzically. "He's tried?"

A short, hollow laugh. "They all try. Sadly they all try."

"What's your dissertation about?"

"Exotics."

"Beg your pardon?"

"Exotics," she said, and a smile painted her lips. "You're not a geologist, are you?"

"I'm a nothing-ologist."

"Exotics are pieces of mountains, more or less, that come from somewhere else. Say that an island arc collides with a continent?" She said it as a question and Tripp found himself nodding. "The continent mass goes down, sinks, and fragments of the islands ride up on top. Couple of million years later I drive up in my Jeep, bang my hammer on that old piece of island, and say that doesn't belong here. That's an exotic."

"An exotic," said Tripp.

"An exotic," she said. "My dissertation's on where you can find them. Continental subduction, abyssal plates, ophiolites, that sort of thing."

"Sounds interesting," said Tripp in a tone he hoped would sound genuine. "But Crossley doesn't like what you've done?"

"Hates it, or at least says he does. Sitting on it."

"Tie it at all to Scott?"

Corry thought about the question for a time. "No direct tie that I can see. He helped with some of the preliminary data. But my pet exotic—the one I'm studying—is an ophiolite over in Idaho that's part of the Laramide Orogeny." A look of bewilderment crossed Tripp's face.

"Sorry," she said. "We do tend to slip into jargon, don't we? What I was trying to say before education got in the way is that my paper has mostly to do with some rocks in Idaho that have nothing to do with Scott's dinosaurs. So no, no tie.''

"You mentioned Donner earlier. Have you had much to do with him?''

"Well, he's around. I had one seminar from him.''

"Ever work for him? Projects, anything like that?''

"Not really. A seminar. Radio-carbon dating. Not much contact with him. I'm more in geology than paleontology.''

"Your impressions of Donner?''

In the background the Caterpillar had stopped and the sounds of the forest were beginning to filter in again. The dog still kept his eyes on Tripp.

"Bit of a jerk, I think.''

"His relationship with Grady?''

"Don't think I'm involved enough to know. Scott had begun to pull a dissertation together when we worked together. And Donner was his faculty adviser on that. I felt that Scott didn't have much respect for him. But I don't recall it ever coming up in an obvious way.'' She uncapped the canteen and gestured to Tripp. This time he nodded and she passed it over. He took a long drink and handed it back. "Nice water," he said.

"Spring water from up above. Best in the world. Loggers haven't gotten there yet.''

Tripp looked at the dog lying at her side. "Loggers don't like your dog much.''

"Blue doesn't like them.''

"Ever run into a guy named John Hunt?''

She laughed pleasantly. "We've crossed paths.''

To Tripp it sounded like a sentence had been left unsaid. "And…?"

Her laugh again. "And, you know what I said about how Grady and I were just friends? Well, maybe John and I took the research a little bit further." The laugh, half-embarrassed now. "He's an old friend."

Tripp nodded. "You said Grady helped you with preliminaries on the dissertation. What exactly?"

"Map searches, mostly. That's what we were working on together."

"Map searches?"

"Yeah. Part of the paper is a survey of all known—or mapped—exotics in the Northwest. Scott and I worked together on that, compiling all the research on northwestern exotics."

"Why Scott's involvement? Friendship?"

She laughed. "You don't know graduate school very well, do you? No, it was a symbiotic relationship. I needed the compilation for my paper. Scott wanted to see if the bone chasers had overlooked any promising areas."

"And?"

"And what?"

"Had they? Overlooked any areas?"

"Oh, I don't know," said Corry. "We never got into discussions of specifics. We'd just ferret out what research had been done, ferret it out independently, and then trade."

"So Scott was looking for new places to hunt dinosaurs?"

"Pretty much," said Corry.

"What became of the research you found, the maps and papers, things like that?"

"We copied off a lot. I've got boxes of it at home."

"And Scott's stuff?"

"Don't know." Corry rose and kicked at the dead ashes of the campfire. The dog rose with her. At length she turned to Tripp. "You think my dissertation's somehow involved in Scott's disappearance?"

Tripp took his time answering. "Hard to say. Lot of little threads out there hanging this way and that. I just haven't figured out yet which one leads to the main string."

"Well," said Corry, "I'm sorry about Scott. But I hope when you find that string, it tugs on Crossley." She pronounced each word exactly and precisely. "He's a nasty man, an evil man."

"Mind if I show you something?" Tripp asked, getting up and retrieving a small notebook from his pickup. "Some of Grady's field notes. That's April. Mean anything to you?"

Corry examined the book page by page. At length she closed it and handed it back. "Is there something there I should know about?"

"Nothing in there rings any bells?" said Tripp. "No notations that look familiar? Anything like that?"

Corry took it back from him and paged through again. "Looks busy," she said. "What's 'J' in here? I see a lot of Js."

"Hum," said Tripp, retrieving the notebook, "good question. Thought you might have some idea. No Js jumping out at you, huh?"

"Nothing."

"Not a shorthand scientific notation, something like that?"

"First I've seen it."

"Anybody you know with that initial? I mean, somebody that would know Grady, too? Initial J?"

Corry's face was blank. "I suppose there are some students with that. But it doesn't really sound like it stands for a name, does it? I mean, he writes in there 'working on J', doesn't he?" Tripp nodded. "If it was a person, would he write 'working on J'? It doesn't sound like that. Working on John? Working on Jane? Sounds more like it stands for some sort of project."

"Nothing jumps out, huh?" Tripp asked again.

"Sorry."

Tripp moved toward the pickup. The dog stood and watched him stiffly. "Good friend you got there."

"Handy to have up in these parts."

"Any chance I could read your dissertation?"

Corry followed him to the truck. "You think it could help?" she asked. "It's pretty dry stuff unless you're in the business."

"Might point to what he was working on."

"Then, sure you can read it. How do I get it to you?"

"Comin' to town any time soon?"

Corry broke into a wide smile. "Take a bath, eat in a restaurant? You bet." She told Tripp how to get in touch with her. "And any news at all on Scott," she said, "find me."

Tripp was thinking again about telephones as he drove away from the clearing. Behind him, Corry Sound and Blue sat at the cold campfire and watched his pickup disappear into the trees.

EIGHTEEN

AFTER A TELEPHONE CHECK with Bowen that all was well with Kathy, Tripp hit the road north again. Driving through the afternoon and evening, he made the motel in Shelby well after midnight. The large frosty woman of before sold him a key, and he crashed for a couple of hours of sleep.

Tripp pulled his truck into the Willow Hills site Wednesday morning just as the first tentative rays of a summer sun were breaking over the eastern plains. The big open-air tent where the sorting and kidding had gone on the week before was deserted, and Tripp found himself wandering out toward the excavation trenches.

"Hey!" A long-haired girl waved from the bottom of a narrow pit. "Welcome back. Changing professions?"

Tripp grinned and returned the wave. It was red T-shirt, who had given him chipping lessons in the dust. "Up awfully early, aren't you?" he said.

"Early pterodactyl gets the polychaete."

"Right," said Tripp. "Looking for Hunt. Know if he's around?"

"Haven't the faintest," she said. "Maybe over there." She pointed off toward another excavation site. "He's usually working the nestings."

Tripp found Hunt flat on his long stomach in one of the taped-off circles they'd visited a week before. Hunt's nose was almost touching one of the porcelain-like spheres as he measured it with a caliper and made notes in a small book.

"Ah, the romantic life of a scientist." Tripp sighed and Hunt looked up.

"And the even more romantic life of a private eye." Hunt grinned. "It's the Big Sleep himself. And what brings himself back to these parts? Kinda early, aren't ya?"

"Couldn't stay away," said Tripp. "The romance, the travel, et cetera, et cetera." They both laughed.

"Long drive for romance," observed Hunt, standing and dusting himself off. Tripp heard it as a question.

"A few loose ends, actually," said Tripp. "Needed to talk to you and Crossley."

"Wow," said Hunt, "your timing's impeccable. Crossley's headed off to Missoula. Probably passed him on the road. We've had a tough week out here."

Tripp remembered Crossley whining about wet-nursing dignitaries. "Yeah, some scientists and an interpreter?"

"Man oh man." Hunt laughed. "It turned out to be a lot worse. Maybe Crossley told you? We were going to have nine people here?"

Tripp nodded.

"Nine turned out to be sixteen," said Hunt. "The four Japanese each brought their own interpreter—and the people from California all brought assistants. Crossley almost had a nervous breakdown. A true circus." Hunt was chuckling.

"So pretty tough on Crossley?"

"Think he'll probably get home, snarl at his wife,

kick his dog, and then get drunk. You said loose ends. Does that mean Grady is back among us?''

"Hardly," said Tripp. "I don't feel like I'm any closer to him than when I saw you last week. No, just some issues came up that I thought I'd try to talk out."

"Well," said Hunt, "what can I do to help?"

Tripp hesitated. John Hunt had known Scott Grady. John Hunt may have had motive, if competition could be construed as motive. And the enigmatic initial J. Tripp decided to proceed carefully.

"Well," Tripp began, "I've talked to pretty much everyone who knows him, including you." Hunt nodded. "And now I'm trying to tie down where people were when he disappeared."

"And that was exactly?"

"The weekend of May 23rd and 24th," said Tripp. "Saturday the 23rd."

"Dead rock-solid easy for me," said the tall man. "I was right here, probably within two feet of where we're standing."

"You didn't have finals?" Tripp asked, feeling pleasantly relieved that the tall man had a good alibi. He'd grown to like Hunt enormously.

"Wasn't involved this year," answered Hunt. "Half dozen of us came up here the week before finals to get the camp set up."

"But I thought Grady was supposed to run it?"

"Specialties," said the tall man. "I'm actually good at getting these things going, so that's what I do—go around and get the various digs set to go, then I take off for my own particular work."

"But you had to stay on here when Grady didn't show?"

"You got that one right."

"Okay," said Tripp. "Another question, if I can?"

"Shoot."

"Where were you a week ago last Monday night?"

"Why?" asked Hunt. "Oh, I can answer that. I was right here. I haven't left this dig for a month, not even a trip into Shelby. Too much to do."

"Does Crossley own a car?"

"I suppose that's one definition of what he drives," said Hunt. "It's more like a bus or small truck. An old Range Rover. Think he keeps it mostly at his place in Great Falls. Drives a state car around here. A state van, actually."

"Seen it up here?"

"Sort of comes and goes. Sometimes he has it, sometimes he doesn't."

"Was Crossley here last Monday? A week ago this past Monday?"

"Wow," said Hunt, pulling his notebook from a rear pocket, "that seems like a year ago." He flipped back through a couple of pages. "No," he said at length. "My notes have me dealing with the water company from Shelby because Crossley was in Great Falls for a meeting."

"Your notes say when he left?" asked Tripp, but he realized it was probably meaningless—whatever Crossley was doing last Monday, his wife said they were in Seattle on the weekend of Grady's disappearance.

"They don't say," answered Hunt, "but that's easy. He left late Sunday—I remember him making a big deal about me getting water tanker service in here, and that was over dinner Sunday. So he left late Sunday."

Behind them a noisy clanging broke out near the tents.

"Breakfast bell," said Hunt. "Hungry?"

"Actually I am," said Tripp. "Room enough for me?"

Hunt laughed. "With the metabolisms we deal with up here, food's one thing we make sure we have plenty of."

Hunt led them to an open-sided tent at the rear of the sorting area where trays of sausage and scrambled eggs were laid out. A couple of sleepy looking kids had already loaded their plates. Tripp and Hunt did the same, and Hunt led them off to the small knoll where they'd talked the first day. They arranged themselves with their faces to the rising sun.

"We found Grady's climbing notes," said Tripp. "The ones he left just in case?" Hunt waited for him to go on. "Nothing for the weekend he disappeared."

"Then he wasn't climbing," said Hunt.

"Or he left a note and somebody took it," said Tripp.

"Possible."

Tripp fished into his hip pocket and produced Grady's field notes from April. He handed them to Hunt.

"Grady's?" said Hunt, leafing back through the pages.

"None for May," offered Tripp.

Hunt studied the small book for a minute.

"That's weird," he said, more to himself than to Tripp.

"What?"

"Well, all the Js."

"Yeah," said Tripp, "we thought that was pretty weird, too. That's one of the reasons I'm up here. Mean anything to you?"

"Well," said Hunt, going farther back into the small book, "it's all the way through here, isn't it? Js almost every day. Even weekends." He handed the book back to Tripp. "Sorry, but I can't say that it means anything to me."

"Not a scientific notation, or something like that?"

Hunt shrugged. "Initial of my first name, I suppose." He looked up at Tripp. "Look, I figured from the start that I was a suspect in this. After all, I know the guy, worked around him. But I didn't do anything to him. I've been up here solid since before he turned up missing. The initial may mean John, but it's not the me John." Hunt's eyes were steady and intense.

"I believe you, John," Tripp said simply. "So what's—or who's—the J?"

"Well," he said finally, "they're in his field book, so that means it's something work related."

"Huh?" asked Tripp, shaking his head.

"Tradition," said Hunt. "The only things that go in field books are work and notes about work. No play in those things. So if it's in there, it's work. Even on a day when you haven't done very much work, it's the last thing you do before you go to bed. Pull out that little book and write it all down."

"You guys find anything important up here

around Christmas? His first J is right around last Christmas.''

"Hardly," Hunt said. "This place is rock-solid closed in December—closed all winter. Ever been up here in the winter?''

"Then what do you think?''

"Maybe he made a laboratory discovery,'' offered Hunt. "I just don't know.''

"And then," said Tripp, "we see J in almost every field note through winter and all the way to the end of April. Ideas?''

"Probably not laboratory work then," said Hunt. "I didn't see him in the lab that much. So maybe fieldwork and writing up whatever it was that was turning his crank.''

"It'd take that much time?" asked Tripp. "We're talking six months.''

"Easily," said Hunt, "if it was something big. The science up here has drifted on for years. Stuff's slow. Everything has to be cross-referenced with everything else that's been done on the subject. You not only do your own science, but you have to know everyone else's.''

Tripp recalled Corry Sound describing the cross-referencing work they'd done together. "I met Corry," he said.

Hunt threw a quick glance toward Tripp. "And…?''

"Nice woman," said Tripp. "Sends her regards.''

Hunt didn't say anything.

"Said she knows you?" Tripp formed it as a question beneath a smile.

"She does.''

"Why do I get the feeling this might be a bad subject?"

Silence for a time. Then: "Well, she sort of dumped me."

Tripp laughed despite himself.

Hunt turned toward him, offended. "That's funny?"

"Well, no," said Tripp. "Just your reaction."

The big man eased up. "Oh well, sometimes you're the dumper, sometimes the dumpee."

"Nice woman," said Tripp. "Interesting dog."

"Blue," said Hunt. "That's one very smart dog. But protective—wow. One of the problems in our brief relationship. Any time I'd try to get a little romantic, that dog'd start growling." They both laughed.

"J, huh?" said Tripp at length. "Well, at least we know he was working…we know that he wasn't letting up. He was working harder than ever, by the look of his notes."

"There's an easy way to find out what he was doing," said Hunt brightly. Tripp looked at him blankly.

"Just read his research. You don't do six months around the clock and not write it down."

"Tried that," said Tripp. "Didn't work. Looked through his office pretty carefully. Not one paper with a this-year date on it."

"Possible," said Hunt, "that he hasn't printed out anything yet. Printout's really the last step."

"Computers?" said Tripp.

"Sure. We do all this stuff on computers. The printing it is just the last step. That and the bows to an admiring world."

"School computers?"

"Except for the mainframe, those things are garbage," said Hunt. "Wouldn't write to my mother on one of those things. No, there's a real arms race among the grad students over computers. Everyone's always trying to get a bigger and faster one and outdo his friends. We all work on our own equipment. Grady does, too."

Tripp thought about his own feeble attempts to get into Grady's computer. "You pretty good on computers?"

Hunt laughed. "They don't call me Nanobite for nothing."

A plan formed in Tripp's mind. "Can you get out of here for a couple of days?"

Hunt shot him a wary look. "I'm not sure there's a precedent."

"We could set one."

"Crossley's gone."

"Then he'll never miss you."

"Where to?"

"Missoula."

Hunt smiled broadly. "Let me grab a toothbrush and my lucky shirt."

NINETEEN

JESSIE HUMBLE didn't look as spry this early Thursday morning as she had a few days before. Her hair uncurled and pinned back, a tattered housecoat thrown around her shoulders, the good landlady looked every one of her eighty-plus years. She opened the door suspiciously but gave Tripp the key when she had figured out who he was. "Leave it as you found it," she ordered. Tripp and Hunt were already climbing the stairs.

The apartment was unchanged from four days before. The same musty smell, same dim light made even dimmer by the early hour.

Hunt seated himself in front of the computer. "Nice machine. Big mother." He fired it up.

Tripp used the phone to call Bowen. His friend had obviously been sleeping.

"Wake up, Nate, for crying out loud," bellowed Tripp. "It's the middle of the day."

"I'm here, I'm here," mumbled Bowen. "What time is it?"

"I'm back in town," said Tripp. "Hunt and I are at Grady's. He's going through the computer."

"You don't think he's our J?"

"Looks doubtful."

"Weird," interrupted Hunt from across the small room.

"What?" asked Tripp, covering the mouthpiece.

"Bunch of stuff's been erased."

"Hunt says stuff's been erased," Tripp said into the phone. "He's working it right now."

"All right," said Bowen in a tone of admiration. "You guys're moving fast."

"What of our friend Wells comma Vernon?" Tripp asked into the phone.

"Nasty little creep, isn't he?" said Bowen. "Chatted him up. A very snaky little guy, if you ask me. Didn't seem to know diddly about J. Told him I didn't believe him. Got a little heated. You know he actually shoved me?"

Tripp laughed despite himself. "You shove back?"

"I'm way too much of a gentleman," replied Bowen. "No, I merely seized his peaked little head and showed him where his nose would be if he ever touched me again." Bowen was awake—he was laughing. "Also checked the airlines. Your cousins the Crossleys were on that flight to Seattle."

Hunt was signaling from across the room.

"I'll be in touch," said Tripp.

"Take a look at this stuff," said Hunt with a trace of astonishment in his voice. Tripp peered over the screen and saw only a couple of long lines of numbers. "So?"

"Somebody erased everything back all the way to May," said Hunt. "May of last year."

"Nothing in there at all from this year?"

"Not a byte. Like somebody went in with a big magnet and just totally wiped everything."

"Maybe he hasn't used it since last May?"

"It's been used. There's usage tracking data for almost every day for the last year. I went back thirteen months. Just no stored data."

"Usage tracking?" said Tripp uncertainly.

"Shows that the machine's been used," said Hunt. "Don't know what it did, but it was used."

"Then we're sunk?"

"Have faith, man," said Hunt. "You've got Nanobite on the case. Give me a break"—he entered in a series of numbers—"and about five minutes."

Tripp sat down and tried to watch quietly, but he couldn't keep his mouth shut. "What're you doing?"

"Mmmm," was all Hunt would say as he worked the keyboard. The screen was flashing through a series of columns.

"Getting anything?"

"For crying out loud. Shut up."

Tripp tried. But it only lasted a few seconds.

"Anything?" he said, almost timidly.

"Almost there," said Hunt, absorbed in the screen.

"You think you can get it?"

Hunt didn't even answer as he continued to choreograph the keyboard.

"Nanobite reigns!" he yelled at last. "Got it, I got it!" He spread his arms wide in front of the computer. "Try to keep me out, huh?" He turned to Tripp. "Don't know what it is exactly, but we've got tracks in the snow. Come on over and have a look-see." He was pointing at the screen. "Now watch." He entered a series of numbers into the machine. "This is all the stuff he's been doing for a year." The computer screen lit up with columns of numbers and letters.

"Almost fourteen million bytes used in all of this," said Hunt, "so it's huge. See, whatever he was working on is gone. But this tracking program is telling us that over the last year the computer used up fourteen million bytes of storage. So we know there was a lot in here.''

''But it's gone?'' asked Tripp, a sinking feeling in his stomach.

''Yeah,'' said Hunt, ''it's gone, whatever it is. But cheer up—it left a trail. Now watch.'' The tall man entered in another string of numerals. The screen came to life with a long series of columns.

''What's that?''

''Umm,'' said Hunt. He keyed in another sequence.

Tripp tried again. ''What's that?''

''Do try to shut up.''

Tripp backed up but kept his eyes on the screen. It flashed through a couple of blank pages, then a long column of numbers came up on the left side.

''Okay, here's the scent,'' said Hunt, pointing to the line of numbers. ''Remember, I think I told you that scientists not only have to do their own work but know everybody else's?''

Tripp nodded.

''Well,'' said Hunt, ''this little number here tells us where Grady was looking to find what others had been doing. Pretty neat, huh? Now watch.'' Another series of entries. The screen came up with another list. ''May, last year,'' said Hunt. ''Grady was hitting the main databases at the school. Not surprising. That's what we all do. Pull up the databases at school and see what research has been done on any particular issue. Okay''—he entered another code— ''now let's move to August. Same databases. And here's a connection to the Smithsonian archives in Washington.''

"Connection?" said Tripp.

"Yeah," said Hunt. "The 202 area code gives it away. We use these numbers all the time." Hunt played with the keyboard. "What he's doing here's pretty simple. You figure out the database you want to search and the computer basically reaches out through the phone, connects with that database, and scans its contents. We all do it all the time. Lets us know what our competition's up to."

"Long distance?" said Tripp. "As in long-distance bills that maybe we can trace?"

"Goes through the university," said Hunt. "No toll costs to the students."

"What's he searching for?"

"Can't get that specific," said Hunt. "I can show you where he looked, not what he looked for. Now"—he entered in a new series—"now let's speed ahead to December. That's when you got the first J, right?"

"Right."

"Okay, here's December usage. First time he writes down J is what date?"

"December 27th."

"Okay," said Hunt. "No computer usage for the 27th. He wasn't on the computer, wasn't doing anything. But here's something the day before that, the 26th. Look at this." Tripp peered at the screen. There were more than a dozen search entries for the day. Grady had used the computer more than a dozen times to get into research files.

"Busy little beaver," said Hunt. "Let's see what he was after." Another line of data. "Same stuff.

Mainframe at the school—that's just the reference stuff we all use. Here's 202—the Smithsonian again. Hmm. Look, here's a query to a 617 area code. That's odd. Harvard databases."

"Unusual?" asked Tripp.

"A little. Good archives. We don't use it much, though, because it's expensive. School has a hernia when they get Harvard bills. Have to really want to know something if you're gonna pay that kind of change." Hunt played with the keyboard.

"What else?"

"Nothing else. Lot of accessing to Harvard. Odd. Look at these two weeks right before Christmas." Hunt had his finger on the screen, counting down the column. "Thirteen calls to Harvard. Wow, I'd get killed if I did that. Two weeks in December, all to Harvard." Hunt hit the keyboard again, his long fingers moving over it like a pianist.

"Scanning into this year." Hunt watched a new screen come up. "Wow! Look at the usage after December...really drops off. Look"—he pointed to a small line of numbers—"it's off to almost nothing. Here's February. Nothing almost. Just two calls to the Smithsonian. Okay, March: two hits again, both to the Smithsonian. No 617. No Harvard. April, again...wait. No, three hits in April. All Smithsonian. Okay, now let's try May." The computer thought for a second, then came up with a new screen. Two lines of numbers. Hunt studied them.

"Weird one this time. Let's see. May. Month he disappears. A call to 202. That's Smithsonian. But here's another 202 I don't know." Hunt read off a ten-digit line of numbers. "Not Smithsonian. Not familiar."

"What is it?" asked Tripp impatiently. "Something?"

"Well, Grady's using it, so let's see. Turn on that modem."

Tripp looked around.

"Little rectangular white box over there," said Hunt, pointing toward the end of the desk.

Tripp fumbled with the device, and a series of red lights flashed back and forth across its face.

Hunt keyed in the phone number. "See what there is to see." The computer digested the numbers and the modem came to life, emitting the sounds of a telephone signal, a ring, then a series of clicks and squeals. Hunt was peering hard at the screen. "We're in," he said. "Wow, that's a weird one."

Tripp bent over Hunt's shoulder. On the screen a meaningless line of letters and numbers. Below it a four-letter prompt: *NCIC>*.

Tripp stepped back. Looked around the room. Focused again on the screen. "N-C-I-C," he said slowly. "National Crime Information Computer." Through his mind flashed the New York newsroom, his old friend, and the long list of names he'd given her to check through the same databases. One hit from that check: John Hunt. From a database you search only if you're looking for crime—or criminals. Why would Scott Grady be trying to get into the national crime computer? "Any way to tell what exactly he was looking for?"

"No indication," said Hunt. "Pretty amazing.

The national crime computer. Wonder if I'm in here.''

"You are," said Tripp neutrally.

Hunt turned, his face serious.

"I had a friend run names," said Tripp.

"That old pot bust?"

Tripp nodded.

"Wow, that's gonna haunt me. That was in here?"

"Cultivation, it said."

"Two stupid plants," said Hunt. "Had 'em on a piece of plywood under a skylight in my bathroom. Some jerk turned me in."

Tripp shrugged and bent over the computer screen. "No way to tell from that what Grady was looking for?"

Hunt shook his head. "None."

"But you think he could get into it?" said Tripp. "I mean, get into the files?"

Another head shake from Hunt. "No way of knowing. I suppose, though. I mean, he was playing with it. He was there." Hunt once again hunched over the keyboard. Tripp watched him work the machine for maybe five minutes. At length, Hunt hit a key and the screen went blank. He turned in his chair. "Think that's it. If there's anything else in there, I can't find it."

Tripp sat on the edge of the bed. "So what've we got?" he said, more to himself than anyone else.

"Tracks in the snow," offered Hunt.

Tripp ran it over in his mind, looking for a pattern—for breaks in pattern. Heavy computer use…the pattern. Something big stored there, then erased. A break in the pattern. Continuing searches through databases up to about Christmas...pattern. Then almost no archival searches after Christmas...a break in the pattern. A summer and fall of accessing the Smithsonian archives...pattern. Then a two-week flurry of hitting the Harvard files. Break in pattern. And then, finally, the single call to the national crime computer. In the same month Grady disappeared. Pattern twisted out of recognition.

Tripp felt tired, overwhelmed. With no certain directions. "What grabs you right now?" he asked his tall friend. "You're in school. You do a lot of the same things Grady does—or did. Anything jump out at you in the computer?"

"Well, the crime computer thing, obviously," said Hunt. "I mean, that comes right out of left field."

Tripp nodded.

"And I guess the Harvard stuff. That rings a bit off to me. I mean, it's a file we use now and then. But man, it's expensive and, you know, it's not like the Smithsonian or something like that. Not something you just sort of casually dial up. I mean, I've used it maybe twice or three times in all the time I've been here. He used it solidly for two weeks in December. That's a bit off."

Tripp stood up and stretched. A wave of exhaustion swept over him. "We're tired," he said. "Let's get some rest. And I've got a date tonight."

Hunt grinned lecherously.

"Don't look so pleased," said Tripp. "It's with your old girlfriend, and you're gonna be there."

TWENTY

"HAVEN'T HAD this big a party since graduation," Bowen said as he moved around the porch, picking up old newspapers and trying to tidy what hadn't been straightened up since the porch was built. "Sure hope there's enough ice."

Kathy laughed from the overstuffed easy chair. "Nathan, it's not a party, for crying out loud. It's a meeting, sort of."

"Feels like a party," he said, the naked overhead bulb exaggerating his angular features. A straight-backed wooden chair creaked as he put his weight on it and pulled himself up to the table. In front of him two piles of paper that Tripp had arranged: the Grady climb notes and the field books. Bowen looked across at Tripp. "Think this is gonna help, Benjamin?"

Tripp shrugged his shoulders.

Headlights crossed the parking area and a dark subcompact pulled in.

"That'd be Hunt," said Tripp, rising from the table and watching the tall man's frame unwind from the car in the near darkness of the lot. Tripp waved, and Hunt swung easily up the steps of the porch as Tripp made introductions.

Hunt surveyed the papers on the table, a troubled look on his face. "Grady's things?"

Tripp nodded. "Thought we might be able to piece things together a bit. Corry's bringing her dissertation. So we might have a better idea of what Grady was chasing.''

"She's coming, then?"

"Called her this morning. Said she'd be here."

"Should be an interesting evening," said Hunt.

Tripp smiled. Another pair of headlights swung into the yard.

Corry Sound had left the high mountains far behind. In the place of the ragged vest and faded jeans she'd chosen an ankle-length lightweight summer dress that fell from her broad shoulders in earthy shades of green and brown. Her blond hair curled in at her neck and subdued makeup brought out the blue of her eyes. Tripp introduced her around. "And of course you know Mr. Hunt, I take it?"

Hunt rose, grinning. Corry stood almost six feet in high heels. Hunt towered above even her. Across the table Kathy seemed lost in the redwood forest of tall humans.

"Charmed," said Corry, holding out her hand to Hunt. "May I call you John?" She laughed as she said it.

"Nice to see you, Cor," he said. Kathy shot Tripp a look of understanding.

"Everybody have drinks?" said Tripp. "Sit and let's get this thing done." Small chat as they all pulled up around the table.

Tripp quickly turned the mood serious. "Think maybe if we do an overview, we might be able to share information and ideas. I guess the way to start is with the notion that we're here because Scott Grady isn't—and because somebody tried to kill Kathy." All eyes around the table turned to her.

"Since then we've been trying to find out who and why."

Kathy picked up the thread, her rich voice steady and controlled. "Scott is—or was, I'm not sure which now—a friend of mine. From the university. He missed a lunch date with me in late May. I tried to find him, couldn't, and went on vacation for several weeks. When I came back he was still gone." She looked across the table at Tripp. "I got worried and went to Ben here."

"We met a week ago Monday at my ranch," said Tripp. "On her way back to town, Kathy was run off the road and nearly killed." Kathy held up her arm in a cast. "Then, last Friday, somebody tried to kill me." Tripp told them about the fire, took a sip of his drink, and looked at Hunt and Sound. "You're here because you might—unknowingly— hold some key to this thing. I've talked to a string of other people associated with Grady. But, frankly, my suspicions about them are too heavy to bring any of them into this."

Tripp outlined what he'd learned of Grady, how so many things about him had changed at Christmas: the growing absences from school and classes, the new references to J in his field notes, how he didn't seem to be mountain climbing as much. "There's a thread in there somewhere," said Tripp, "and maybe we can find it." He turned to Corry. "Any of this mean anything to you?"

Corry shook her head. "We'd pretty well wrapped things on that part of my dissertation by October," said Corry. "By Christmas, let's see, I guess we hadn't worked together in two or three months."

Tripp pushed the stack of notebooks to the center of the table. "Grady keeps good notes. All through last year, they're just regular field notes, though. Digging in this, doing that. Then right at Christmas, they change. Suddenly they're sprinkled with references to something called J. Mean anything to anybody?" The table was silent.

Tripp continued. "John and I went into Grady's computer this morning. All the data he'd stored there—and there was a huge amount of it—all that data has been erased."

"Everything he'd done on his dissertation?" asked Corry.

"Everything gone," said Hunt.

"And again," said Tripp, "we see patterns somehow being interrupted. Nanobite here"—he glanced at Hunt—"Nanobite did manage to pull up some stuff. Usage records, that sort of thing. Up to about Christmas, everything looks pretty normal. Grady's using the machine to pull up reference files at the clip of one or two a day, with a few days off for climbing. Then right at Christmas the pattern changes. From there until this last May he's only hitting the archives maybe once or twice a month."

"Maybe he'd completed his research," said Corry. "I mean, that's sort of the way you do it. You compile and compile and compile. Then, after you've got the base research, you stop compiling and start writing." She looked around the table. "That's the way I do it."

Hunt spoke up. "Me, too, actually. So maybe that's not a big deal."

"Maybe not," agreed Tripp. "But isn't it kind

of a weird coincidence that everything turns at Christmas?" He looked around the table.

"Coinkydink," said Kathy, then looked up, startled that she'd said it. "Sorry."

"What?" said Tripp.

"Just something a friend used to say when there wasn't much of an explanation for things. Coinkydink. Coincidence." She took a self-conscious sip of her drink.

"I brought my dissertation," said Corry. "I'll get it." She rose and left the table. Bowen played with the notebooks. Kathy's eyes were on the darkened tree line by the river.

"'Fraid it's pretty scientific," said Corry as she returned, dropping a plastic-bound report the size of a thin magazine on the table. Corry glanced at Tripp. "Help yourself."

Tripp picked it up and read the title aloud. *"A Pico Terrane-Specific Survey of Ophiolitic Serpentines in the Laramide Orogeny."* He made a wry face.

Corry laughed. "Don't be too put off. Means a survey of green rocks in the Rockies, or words to that effect."

Tripp handed it to Hunt. "Maybe you could do the honors?"

Hunt took the paper and began quietly paging through it, glancing up occasionally to ask Corry a question. Bowen got fresh drinks. Kathy moved behind Tripp and laid her good hand casually on his shoulder. Tripp covered her hand in his. Her skin felt smooth and cool. He vowed silently that when this whole thing was over, he was going to get to know her a lot better.

At length, Hunt laid the report on the table and looked at Corry. "Nice stuff," he said and she nodded thanks. "Very nice stuff. How much of this did Grady contribute?"

Corry took the report from him, opening it to a back page and spreading it on the table. "Mostly this kind of thing," she said, pointing to a map of Oregon. "We did state-by-state maps for the whole Northwest pinpointing exotic terranes."

Kathy broke in. "Exotic whats?"

"Exotic terranes," said Corry. "Mostly—well, not all the time—but mostly it's rock where you don't expect to find it. Old sea floors, things like that that have been pushed up and sort of stranded in other formations. See. Here's Idaho." She tapped her painted fingernail on a spot in the northern part of the state. "This's the area my dissertation's on. Ancient sea floor that pushed in over the continental landmass and got cut off there. A bunch of alien rock surrounded by batholithic granite." She flipped to another map. "Washington. Here's Montana."

"Can I see?" said Hunt, turning the map around so it was right side up to him. Tripp watched as Hunt's long finger traced out shaded areas on the map. "Strange," he said.

"What?" asked Tripp. "What's strange?"

"Lot of stuff in the Bitterroot Mountains south of here that I wasn't aware of. Look." Hunt turned the map and Tripp inspected it, following the route of the Bitterroot River south and picking out the mountains to the west. Little eraser-sized patches throughout the range had been shaded in light blue.

"Can I see?" Corry took the paper from him and studied the map. "That's mostly Scott's work," she

said. "He focused a lot on the Bitterroots. Turns
out there's quite a bit of ophiolitic material in
there."

"Abyssal or littoral?" said Hunt.

"Both," said Corry. "But I think there's quite a
bit of littoral."

"Wow," said Hunt, but quietly and to himself.

"What?" said Tripp. "Why 'wow'?"

"Bit of a headline." Hunt peered at the map for
fully a minute before he spoke again. "Basically it
boils down to this: We've always known there's lots
of limestone in the Montana mountains, but not the
kind of limestone that could have fossils in it. Looks
like Grady might have found a lot of new rock to
explore." He looked at the map again. "Maybe fossil rock, maybe not. But it's pretty intriguing."

Tripp turned it over in his mind. "So we have
Grady maybe discovering a whole new area for re-
search, a new place to look for fossils. But if the
timing's right, he found that what? Last summer?"
Corry nodded. "And he disappears this May."
Tripp looked around the table. "Connections?"
Blank looks and fidgets.

Tripp thought about the computer session with
Hunt and ran the patterns over in his mind. Grady's
computer calls to the databases slowed dramatically
just after Christmas. The two graduate students at
the table in front of him had an explanation for it:
Grady had done his research and had begun to
write. But that didn't explain the two weeks of calls
to the Harvard files, calls Hunt had found unusual.
Tripp worked a hunch.

"Can I?" said Tripp, leaning over and taking the
dissertation from Corry. "You have a bibliography

in back?'' Corry nodded. Tripp flattened the paper out on the table. The others watched him closely as he ran his finger down the column of research entries. He looked up at Corry. ''No entries from Harvard?''

''Didn't use them,'' Corry said. ''Expensive. I used Smithsonian stuff, mostly. And there just isn't much in the Harvard files on this area—wouldn't do me a lot of good to get into the Harvard material. Stuff in there's real old and pretty outdated, what there is of it.''

Tripp looked at Hunt. Hunt looked back.

Kathy broke in. ''What?''

''Weird,'' said Tripp. ''Maybe it's something, maybe not. But weird.''

The four around the table watched him silently.

''Okay,'' said Tripp, ''I'll try to lay it out. We read Corry's dissertation tonight and discover that Scott is nosing around an area that could be a whole new dinosaur hunting ground. His research and Corry's has found some promising leads—new rock where there could be fossils. I assume that'd be important, John?''

''Could be,'' said Hunt. ''Always looking for new beds. New beds mean new fossils and maybe new answers.''

Tripp nodded. ''We got into Grady's computer enough today to track his research. Matches pretty well with Corry's. Lots of calls all last year to the Smithsonian.''

''That's where we got the Bitterroot stuff,'' said Corry. ''That was mostly Smithsonian data. And that was pretty much Scott's research, his material. I concentrated on Idaho.''

Tripp nodded again. "So he finds some interesting references to the Bitterroots. Finds that there may be some fossil beds out there that people have overlooked. Does the research in the computer. Then I bet he goes out on foot to see if the deposits he found in the research were the kind of beds that hold dinosaur bones. That's all the climbs we see in the Bitterroots."

Hunt spoke up. "But the computer indicates his research went on a long time after he was through with Corry's work."

Tripp picked up the thread. "So he's still gnawing at the bone, so to speak. Even after he's stopped working with Corry, he keeps looking. Something out there is intriguing him. Something in the Bitterroots. Keeps plowing into the Smithsonian files to find new areas. Climbing all the time. Then December."

Hunt spoke up. "Found two weeks solid of Grady getting into the Harvard archives. The two weeks just before Christmas. Had to be looking for the same stuff."

Tripp jumped in. "Betcha he exhausted all the leads he got from the Smithsonian. So now he's looking to see if the old material from Harvard has anything that the Smithsonian doesn't. Material on that kind of rock in the Montana mountains, the dinosaur rock." Tripp paused to collect his thoughts. "Then, the final Harvard entry. December 26th. No more Harvards after that. Either he'd given up—or he found what he wanted. Betcha he found it. The next day, December 27th, we get the very first use of the 'J' in the field notes." Tripp felt his stomach tighten with excitement. "I'm sure of it.

Grady found something in the Harvard archives on the 26th. Then he went out there on foot the next day, the 27th. That's the first use of J. He'd discovered J."

"And everything changing after that." It was Kathy who spoke quietly, wonder in her voice.

"Everything changing after that," echoed Tripp. "He found something that changed him profoundly."

"Question is," said Kathy, "what'd he find?"

"Figure that out," said Tripp, "and I think we figure it all out."

Across the table Hunt grinned broadly and put his arm around Corry. "If Grady can find it," he said, "Nanobite can find it. Science lab, mainframe computer. Eight a.m. Be there. Aloha."

Tripp looked back out toward the river, wondering if Grady had found something important enough to die for.

Grady found something in the Harvard databases that
Libby Twin Angels in the ... Had lanes ...

TWENTY-ONE

THE TALL Hunt was deep into the machine by the
time Tripp made his way to the school's main computer room the next morning. He grunted a small
welcome as Tripp came up beside him. In front of
him a computer screen showed a map painted in
bright artificial blues and reds.

"How's it going?" Tripp's voice was subdued.
He felt close, as if things were about to break open.

"Going," said Hunt. "I'm in the Harvard files,
at least." He pushed a mouse across a pad and the
video map moved right to left.

"Anything?"

"Not yet," said Hunt. "Just got in. Hold on a
sec." The large man moved the cursor across the
screen and keyed the mouse. The map changed to
a series of black and white undulating lines.

"Contour map," said Hunt. "Twin Angels in the
Bitterroots." Hunt moved the cursor. "Nothing obvious." He clicked the mouse and the screen
changed back to the original red and blue map.

"So, talk to me," said Tripp.

Hunt leaned his long frame back in the chair.
"Trying to run comparisons," he said. "Working
on two assumptions. One is that Grady searched
through the Smithsonian files but didn't find what
he was looking for. Other assumption is that he
found something he cared about in the Harvard databases, probably the right kind of rock that might

have fossils. So I'm telling the computer to compare the two and let me know what Harvard has that the Smithsonian doesn't.''

"Machine can do that?" Tripp told himself he had to get computer literate.

"Tricky, but doable. Thinking about it right now. Problem is there are sedimentary beds like this all over Montana. So the two databases have a lot of material in common. Taking awhile."

Tripp pulled a chair up next to him. Along the counter three more computer screens sat dark. Behind them a line of mainframe control units clicked and glowed.

At length the screen in front of Hunt automatically switched from the colored map to a column of figures and then resolved into a series of paragraphs, each about a half dozen lines long.

"Bingo." Hunt traced down the first graph with his finger. "This is the stuff Harvard has that the Smithsonian doesn't." He groaned. "There's a ton of it. Look"—Hunt gestured to the screen, where page after page of information was scrolling through—"must be a hundred entries."

"And it's what?" asked Tripp.

"Basically it's bits and patches of land all around the state where it's possible you might find some fossil remains. Right kind of rock for fossils. Nothing definite, just possibles." Hunt watched the graphs scroll through.

"Then we have to eliminate," said Tripp, "narrow it down. Get rid of the stuff that wouldn't have mattered to him." Tripp got up and paced across the room. Then back, looking over Hunt's shoulder. "Try this, John. Try this on for size. Grady went

out and climbed only on the weekends, right?"
Hunt nodded. "Sometimes he'd spend the night?
Sometimes it was just a day trip? And he seemed
focused on the Bitterroot Mountains, right?" Hunt
nodded again.

"So it has to be within a reasonable driving distance. Say a hundred miles or so of here—and probably in the Bitterroots. Can you narrow that search
to within one hundred miles of here?"

"Easy," said Hunt. "Roughly sixty-six miles to
a degree. So figure we tell the computer to show us
all the areas where there might be fossils within a
degree and a half radius of Missoula." Hunt went
back into the computer. It chewed on the new information for no more than ten seconds before another screen came back up. "Bingo!" said the big
man, his voice tight, serious. "Three hits. We've
got three hits."

Tripp peered over Hunt's shoulder at the screen.
Three lines of numbers.

Hunt keyed in a command. Instantly the screen
changed: three paragraphs.

"What is it?" said Tripp.

"Patch of rock in the Garnets near Drummond.
Ophiolitic. Probably a limestone. No way of knowing whether it's got fossils, but it's the right kind
of sediment."

Grady's old climb notes flashed through Tripp's
mind. One climb in the Garnets. He didn't remember the date, even the month. "What else?"

"Two in the Bitterroots," said Hunt. "Pretty
close together. Wow, this is hot."

"Where?"

"Kootenai Creek," said Hunt. "Thirty miles

south of here. Right kind of rock. Could be fossils."
He turned from the screen. "What d'ya think,
Ben?"

Tripp stepped back. He felt wound tight, on the
edge. The dots were beginning to crowd together.
And the picture emerging showed that Grady had
found something. Something important. The dots
pointed to a stretch of mountains. Find what Grady
had found and, maybe, you find out what happened
to him.

Tripp turned to Hunt. "Can you get a map of the
area?"

"Printing now."

"Want to go for a stroll?"

Hunt nodded, his face grim.

TWENTY-TWO

THE TWO MEN were quiet as they drove fast out of the city. Hunt clutched the computer-generated map in his hand. Their route followed the highway south as it paralleled the Bitterroot River and snaked through farmland and occasional foothills. On the eastern edge of the valley, the Ruby Mountains showed vast bald patches where loggers had clear cut the timber and burned the scrub. Tripp pictured Corry's rough camp in the canyons beyond. To the west the Bitterroots rose in majestic cascades of granite and pine, their treeless peaks still covered in snow.

Past Florence, the highway edged up closer to the mountains, and the pickup cut through stands of heavy timber and old homesteads carved from the forests.

With Hunt navigating, Tripp turned onto a dirt road that led directly up the western foothills. Before them loomed the open face of a large canyon. Kootenai Creek.

At the end of the road a rough parking lot cut from the forest marked where private lands stopped and the federal wilderness area began. No motorized vehicles allowed beyond. No electricity, no phones. The lot was deserted.

Hunt was scanning his map even as Tripp locked up the truck. "First area should be just off a little lake about four miles up. Four miles, four and a half maybe. Map looks like it's up a bit. Maybe have to climb. Second area's about eight miles farther up.''

They fell into single file on the trail, Hunt leading, Tripp having trouble matching the tall man's stride. The trail ran directly beside a rushing stream for almost a mile before gaining some elevation and meandering along the lower slopes of a cliff face for another mile more. At the mouth of a small meadow the two men paused briefly to catch their breath and drink from the icy snow melt. Beyond the meadow the trail again paralleled

the stream. Tripp could feel in his legs that they were climbing steadily.

After almost an hour and a half, the trail broke into a clearing. Beyond, a mountain lake reflected blue and silver under a cloudless noonday sun.

''North Lake of the Kootenais,'' said Hunt, breathing hard from the hike and the thin air. ''Our area should be off about half a mile or so to the right. Time for a break.''

Tripp threw himself down heavily next to the narrow beach. At 9,000 feet he was finding that breathing had become a conscious act. He rubbed cold water across his face.

Hunt was back into the map. ''Shows the band of possible fossil rock somewhere around a pretty big vertical,'' he said. ''Face looks like it might be five hundred or eight hundred feet high. Pretty good pitch. Can't tell from the map exactly where.''

When they'd caught their breath Hunt picked a tortured path snaking north away from the lake. For almost half an hour the two fought through heavy scrub, thorns, and deadfalls before finally breaking

into the clear. Directly in front an enormous cliff
climbed straight up the mountain, its face broken
only by a few narrow ledges and faults.

"Oh man," said Tripp, panting for breath,
"we're not climbing that, are we?"

"Don't know," said Hunt, his eyes drifting up
the sheer rock. "Map's not specific enough. But
even if it's the top"—he gestured to a long break
in the face over toward their right—"there's some
sort of path or chimney over there that looks like it
could take you all the way up without ropes."

The men studied the sheer face.

"Need to split up," said Hunt, "cover more
ground." Tripp managed to nod. "I'll head east,
you west. If you get anything, holler."

"What am I looking for?" asked Tripp.

"Could be almost anything," said the tall man,
"but usually it's a different colored patch of rock.
Should be pretty big, you know, two to three hundred yards across. If it's true dinosaur rock, should
be what we call Morrison formation. Pattern's easy
to spot: our nation's colors—red, white, and blue.
That's Morrison banding. It'll stick out like a sore
thumb in this orange granite."

Hunt moved east, Tripp moved west, picking his
way carefully through the rocks and snagging brush
as he scanned up and down the cliff face. After two
or three hundred yards his neck was aching and he
sat for a minute to ease the cramping. Looking back
up, a spot of light blue caught the corner of his eye.
He focused. Light blue, and next to it red, and then
white. A distinct band maybe 500 feet up the cliff
face. Red, white, and blue. He was standing for a
better look when a scream—"Tripp!"—echoed like

a ricochet through the canyon wall. A rush of adrenaline pounded through Tripp's body as he scrambled across the rocks and deadfalls.

Hunt was standing at the head of a small slope of rocky debris that had weathered off the cliff. Tripp followed Hunt's gaze down over an outcropping of rocks, down across a narrow talus, down to a small area of debris. A torn human leg protruded from the shattered rocks.

Tripp approached the body carefully, a heavy quiet in the air. "Think we found Grady," he said nervously.

The leg ended in a scuffed leather climbing shoe. The rest of the body lay in an impossible contortion, its lethal fractures hidden in torn blue jeans and a shredded nylon jacket. The face had been crushed in the fall, and it appeared that parts had been gnawed at by animals.

Hunt had come up quietly to Tripp's side. The big man's face was pale and he was trembling. He turned away and vomited.

"Grady?" asked Tripp when the big man had recovered.

"Has to be," said Hunt slowly. "Tough to say in that condition. His jacket, though. Yeah, it's Grady. Oh, Jesus."

Tripp sat back on the rocks and stared absently at the body as images and feelings from the past week flashed across his mind. His initial meeting with Kathy, the wreck, the attack in his barn, the growing conviction that Grady was dead. Now his hunch proved out in front of him in ripped flesh and broken bone. One question answered in mortal certainty. Grady is dead. Other questions still hanging on the silent mountain air. Tripp felt his gaze wander up the cliff face.

Hunt followed his gaze. "Bad cliff. Stupid place to climb without ropes."

Tripp looked around at his tall friend. "How do you know he wasn't on ropes?"

"He'd have a climbing harness on," said Hunt, "the harness that ties him into the ropes. Guy was climbing without a rope." Hunt turned his face away, and Tripp realized his friend hadn't been around death before.

"I need to search the body," Tripp said. "Why don't you go back up the slope and see what you can find? Gear, anything like that." Hunt nodded and turned back up the slope.

The body was stiff. Tripp delicately unzipped the nylon windbreaker and felt through its pockets. A few chips of fossil rock and a half-eaten candy bar. Closing his mind to the task, Tripp searched through Grady's pants. In front, a set of keys and some change. A pocket knife and six one-dollar bills. In a rear pocket, a wallet. Tripp opened it. Scott Stanford Grady. In the other pocket a small blue notebook. Grady's field notes.

Hunt came storming down the slope, rocks skittering from beneath his feet. "Got something, Ben, and it's weird." He was carrying a blue backpack and two coils of red nylon rope. "Found it just at the foot of the cliff. Spooky, man. It's all his field gear. A hammer and chisel, some brushes, the stuff he'd use on a dig." Hunt laid the gear on the rocks and the two men looked it over.

"But I found climbing gear in his apartment," said Tripp.

"Probably bought new stuff. But this is weird. I mean, the ropes." Hunt held one up. "Scattered around the base of the cliff. Separate, like they'd come down with him. But this was still in his pack." Hunt held up a thick nylon climbing harness hooked with the same kind of hardware Tripp had seen in Grady's apartment. Only this seemed newer. "It was still in the pack, Ben," said Hunt. "The ropes were outside, scattered on the rocks. Like he'd slipped and come down, ropes and all. But his harness was still in the pack. He'd be wearing it if he was on ropes. He wasn't wearing it." Hunt's expression was grave. "Can't have it both ways."

"Somebody helped him fall?" said Tripp in a low voice.

Hunt nodded grimly. "Has to be."

Tripp turned from the cliff and looked at Grady's body in the rubble. "Somebody threw him off the cliff, and then threw his gear off. To make it look like a fall?"

Hunt nodded. His face was pale.

Tripp looked back up the sheer rock surface. "Remote, out of sight. Perfect place to kill. Make it look like an accident." He started walking toward the cliff. "Think I saw the dinosaur rock up there. You said there's a way up this thing?"

The two men climbed steadily, moving up from rock to rock inside a broad fracture in the face of the cliff. Tripp tried to concentrate on what he was doing, but his mind kept slipping back to Grady's body in the rocks. He had found something up here, probably around Christmas. Came out here all through the winter and the spring to work on it. Then in late May somebody followed him here and

killed him, shoved him to his death from the cliff.
But why? And who? Faces swam through Tripp's
mind: Crossley—probably in Missoula even now—
but alibied, not a possible. Helen Crossley alibied
on the same plane ticket. Vernon Wells—no alibi
and a possible motive. And Howard Donner—no
obvious motive, and he had lied about where he was
the day Grady disappeared. Tripp thought about Kathy. Safe for the moment hidden out at Bowen's.
But a killer was still on the loose, and Tripp
couldn't keep her hidden forever. Vernon Wells
wouldn't dare go up against Bowen. Howard Donner might, but he was in London for two weeks.
Tripp's mind flashed back on Grady's body in the
rocks and he felt a chill.

At length, the crevice spilled out onto a ledge that
narrowed to a few feet in some places, widened to
more than thirty feet in others. The two men rolled
onto it.

"Catch your breath," wheezed Hunt. "Let me
see what's here." He crawled off with a crablike
motion and disappeared around a large outcrop of
rock. Tripp sat for a few moments staring off across
the mountain peaks toward the horizon.

"Tripp! Tripp!" Hunt's yell bounced brittlely
around the granite canyons. "Get over here!"

Beyond the outcrop, Hunt was pointing at a hole
in the cliff face about two feet across. Tripp crawled
up and peered inside. A large cavity had been chiseled out of the soft rock. Toward the back, the un-
mistakable form of a long skeleton. The same kind
of bone he'd seen at Willow Hills.

"And?" said Tripp.

Hunt was beginning to cackle, a crazed slant in

his eyes. "And!" he yelled excitedly. "And!!? Just the whole shooting match, the whole thing, king of the heap! Yahoo!" His voice bounced around the canyons.

"What is it?" Tripp demanded.

"Remember," said Hunt, breathlessly, his words pouring out as if they'd been shot from a machine gun, "remember when I told you about the search for the proof? The proof of warm-bloodedness? Well, boyo boyo boyo, here she be!" He let out another whoop in the still mountain air. "Here she be! A whole fossil! All the soft tissue—everything! It's there! Grady did it! He did it! Grady found himself the Holy Grail!" The tall man sat back on his haunches and laughed hysterically.

Tripp pushed back into the small hole. The dirt under his feet had been torn up and then tamped down, as though it had been walked on repeatedly. In the cut Tripp could make out four large riblike bones. A hole had been chiseled into them. Inside, a nondescript-looking lump of gray-colored stone.

Hunt was behind him, peering over Tripp's shoulder. "Organs," he said, excitedly. "Looks like it's probably lungs. Maybe liver, but probably lungs. But it's soft tissue. Can't be anything else. Wow." He gave off a low whistle.

Tripp backed out and wedged himself around to sit with his legs dangling out over the cliff face. Hunt squatted down next to him.

"The Holy Grail," said Tripp softly, almost to himself. Through his mind swam images of the Willow Hills dig, the nested duckbill eggs, Hunt's comments about rising to the top with the right kind of science. "John," he said, "you mentioned the right kind of science once. The kind that could take somebody to the very top? This the right kind of science?''

Hunt was nodding even before the sentence was out. "The biggest, Ben. Doesn't get any bigger. In our line of work, probably the biggest discovery there's ever been. It is the Holy Grail.''

"Enough to kill for?''

The question seemed to stop Hunt. He looked from Tripp's face to the hole and back to Tripp. "If you're a killer, maybe.''

"Or if you're a professor who'd do anything to get to the top," said Tripp, more to himself than to his friend. "Only two people fit that, John. Carl Crossley and Howard Donner.'' Tripp let the names die out on the breeze. "And only one killed him. That Saturday in May. Crossley's on a plane to Seattle. Donner says he's at a meeting in Idaho. Crossley tells the truth. But Donner lies. The mad Howard Donner who hasn't had an original idea in his life now owns the most significant discovery in dinosaur hunting ever made.''

Hunt tossed a small rock over the ledge. It was a long time before it hit bottom.

Tripp thought of his meeting with Donner in the split-level house over the city. His dramatic pose before the tall windows, his continual warnings about Crossley, about Grady's suicidal nature. All designed to throw him off the scent. There'd be a small welcoming committee at the airport when he returned, and Tripp vowed to be in it.

"Come on, John," said Tripp tiredly, Kathy's face floating in his thoughts. "Let's get this to the police.''

Back down at the bottom of the cliff, Tripp gathered up Grady's wallet and the pack. Nearby lay the notebook he had put aside when Hunt found the ropes. Tripp sat on the rocks and paged through it. Suddenly his stomach lurched.

"Last entry's May twenty-first," he said, without looking up, his voice tight. "That's Thursday, John, not Friday!"

Tripp had scrambled to his feet and was running wildly down the slope. "We've gotta move, John, and fast!"

TWENTY-THREE

BOWEN TOOK THE KEY from Kathy's hand and unlocked the front door.

"Light's just to the right," she said behind him.

Bowen switched on the lamp and surveyed the small room carefully. An African tribal mask above crossed spears stared back blindly from the wall. The air was stale, enclosed. "Stay here," he ordered, moving through the doorway into the kitchen. He turned on the light.

"Bedroom's down the hall," said Kathy. She heard the floorboards creak as Bowen made his way through the hallway. More lights came on. At length, she heard his steps returning.

"Seems fine," he said, but his big face was tight, worried. "Look, Tripp would have a stroke if he knew we were doing this."

"I don't need much, Nathan. Please." Her voice had taken on a determined tone. She pushed past him into the kitchen. "We're here. It's fine. Give me an hour. Okay? I know you won't even leave the front curb. But one hour? Please. Just give me that much space?"

"Tripp'll know if he comes by the store," said Bowen. "I left him a note. This is stupid."

"Then he'll have to blame it on me," said Kathy implacably.

Bowen's big form was wedged in the kitchen doorway. "I checked the locks and the back door.

Checked the windows. Nobody's been in. And everything's locked.''

Kathy nodded. "It looks the way it did when Ben and I were here. It's okay, Nathan. Just one stupid hour alone? If I'm not worried you shouldn't be either.''

"One hour then," said Bowen. "I'm gonna be right outside in the car. And I'm back in here in one hour.''

Bowen made his way to the front door. "Lock this behind me.''

He stepped outside. Kathy closed the door. The latch turned.

A streetlight cast a bluish circle on the corner. And a soft wind had come up out of the west, carrying the smells of river bottom and pine. No stars out. Clouds. Probably rain.

Bowen moved quietly down the narrow walkway to his car, the weeping willow rustling gently to the side. As he slid the key into the ignition, he heard a soft movement behind him. The big man turned quickly, but not quickly enough as something black and heavy smashed like steel into the side of his face. Bowen fought for consciousness, but the weight crashed down again and he slumped into darkness.

Strong hands pulled Bowen's inert form into the passenger seat. A man climbed behind the wheel, a key turned in the ignition, and the car moved down the street and turned the corner. A dark arm holding something heavy swung down again toward Bowen's face.

THE STORE was closed, the lights were off as Tripp and Hunt swung into Bowen's. The back porch was deserted and Bowen's Jeep was gone.

"Nathan! Kathy!" Only silence answered Tripp's calls. He ran into the kitchen and then the front of the store. Empty.

"Tripp!" It was Hunt yelling from the porch. "Tripp! A note!"

Tripp ran out onto the porch and grabbed the sheet of paper. Lunging down the steps, he shouted back at Hunt: "Call the police! Kathy's house. Sullivan. I don't know the address. It's on Gerald. Hurry!"

Tripp fishtailed the pickup out of the parking lot and squealed rubber as he hit the highway. Through his mind swirled the twisted body of Scott Grady. And the small notebook. No note for Friday, May 22nd—he hadn't had a chance to write it. Grady'd died on Friday, not Saturday as Tripp had assumed. Tripp cursed at himself for missing the obvious. Friday. Not Harry Donner—he'd been in Idaho all day Friday. Friday. In Tripp's mind loomed another face that filled him with hatred and dread—the face of the diminutive dinosaur hunter, the little man with the big ego who always finished second, the courtly professor who'd assured him Grady had "gone down the road." The face of Carl Crossley—somewhere right now in town. Tripp feared he knew where, and he pushed the pickup until the engine was screaming.

KATHY HEARD Bowen's Jeep pull away as she was taking the cork from a bottle of white wine. She poured half a glass and wandered back into the living room.

"Nice little house," she said, looking around at the shelves of books and the mask on the wall. She felt almost giddy to be home. "Missed you, little house."

She knelt in front of the stereo and found a disc. A soft Irish air filled the room. She lay back on the sofa and sipped the wine, closed her eyes.

"Irish, isn't it?"

Kathy started so hard the wine splashed across her jeans. In the kitchen doorway, a short, solid man. On his hands, plastic surgical gloves. In one of them a pistol. Pointed at her face.

"Love Irish music," the man said. "Has a soul, a history that's almost palpable."

Kathy started from the sofa.

"No!" barked the man menacingly as he took two steps into the room. "Stay. Yes, that's a good dog." He laughed softly. "Yes, do stay."

Kathy searched his face, her eyes wild.

"We've not met," said the man, bowing ever so slightly from the waist. "I'm Carl Crossley. We've spoken on the phone, though." He smiled and it terrified her.

"What do you want?" she managed to stammer.

"You dead, I'm afraid." He grinned and the little mustache bunched at the corners of his mouth. Keeping the gun trained on her face, Crossley moved into the center of the room.

"Brought you a present, love." He reached into the breast pocket of his khaki shirt and pulled out a folded piece of paper. He threw it at her and Kathy ducked back.

His voice lashed her like a whip. "Read it!"

Her hands trembling to the point where she could
barely use them, Kathy unfolded the paper.

"Read it!"

Kathy glanced down. It was a poem. Like the
poems she'd gotten from Wells. A centered title, his
name, a few lines of verse.

"Now!" shouted Crossley. "Read it!"

"'A Poem on Passing,'" she began, but her voice
failed and tears blurred the page.

Crossley snatched it from her.

"A lovely work," he sneered as he held it up.
"Your dear little Vernon's last words to you. 'A
Poem on Passing.' Like the other garbage you've
got tucked away in your closet."

Kathy looked toward the kitchen door.

Crossley followed her gaze. "Oh, I've read the
vomit"—Crossley seemed to spit the word at her—
"the vomit he's sent you. Tucked in your little
closet. You like his poetry?" Crossley edged toward the mantel.

Kathy shook her head. "What…what do you
want?"

"You dead. I think we're being redundant now.
You dead."

"Why?" Her question came out hoarse and low,
almost a croak.

"Inevitability, I suppose. There's just too much
you know—or let me restate that: There's too much
you appear to know." With the gun leveled
squarely at her head, Crossley groped beside himself across the mantel. A framed picture crashed to
the floor, its glass shattering. Kathy jumped.

Crossley grabbed a small fossil and held it out to
her. "Missing any of these?" Kathy looked at him

blankly. "Missing any *rocks,* are you, dear?" Crossley laughed. "No, I suppose you wouldn't say, would you?"

"You killed Grady." It was a statement of fact from Kathy.

"Ah, go for the gold, young lady. Of course I killed Grady. As I think you well know."

"Why?"

"Because he was piggishly selfish. Because of his discovery, an enormous discovery. A discovery young Scott refused to share. With the man who made him what he was, what he would have someday been. If he had been more generous."

Kathy fought to control her breath. "But why me?"

"Oh please, don't play the idiot."

"Please," said Kathy. The word came from her lips like a low moan. "Why me?"

TRIPP PULLED his pickup to the end of Kathy's block, the engine idling in the quiet night. Beyond, a streetlight cast a bluish cone across the corner intersection. The house looked peaceful. The blinds were drawn, but Tripp could see light peeking out. Something, though, felt wrong, somehow out of place. Tripp cruised slowly down the street. Near the end of the block Tripp glanced off to his right. There, around the corner, Bowen's Jeep. Tripp pulled up behind it. It looked deserted. Tripp approached it cautiously and gasped as he saw Bowen's slumped form through the window. He yanked the door open and reached across to his friend. Bowen's head was matted in blood and his breathing was low and shallow. Quickly Tripp felt along his neck for a pulse. It was there. "I'll be back, partner."

Killing his light, Tripp guided his pickup quickly to the next intersection and did a U-turn. Coming back down past the Jeep, he continued on straight, past Kathy's street, to the next street over. He turned left, slowed. Cars along the curb. Quiet houses beyond darkened lawns. Near the end of the street a battered and dirty Range Rover. Crossley's car. Tripp pulled up behind it and killed the engine.

"ENOUGH ALREADY," said Crossley. He was tossing the fossil rock casually up and down in his free hand. The other hand held the gun steady on Kathy's face. "When Grady told me he had insurance, that he put the evidence in a safe place, the bull's-eye descended on you, my dear professor. What safer place than his philosopher girlfriend, eh?" Crossley let out a low chuckle. "I suspected you knew. When you called me that Monday after he disappeared, I suspected. And I would've killed you then, but you left town. And then I had to leave town."

Kathy's eyes were locked on the surgical gloves and the gun just inches from her face.

Crossley laid the rock back on the mantel. "Did Scott ever actually tell you about the special rock he gave you? The rock that sat for months up here on your mantel?"

"They were just rocks," cried Kathy.

"Hardly." Crossley laughed. "One wasn't just a rock. More a piece of the future."

Kathy looked at him, terror and bafflement in her eyes.

"Too bad you never knew. Would've made your death a little more worthwhile. Scott found the mother lode of fossils, the kind of thing that will turn science upside down. He was worried"—Crossley laughed—"and it turns out rightfully so, he was worried that I'd try to share in it. So he left a chunk of it with you. For safekeeping? I found it shortly after I killed him. Broke in when you weren't home. Found the rock. And got rid of it."

"It was you?"

"Indeed. But since I found it, you had to die. You might have known."

"But I didn't," cried the woman.

"More's the pity. Enjoy your little near-lethal spin into Pattee Canyon? I've had the dents removed."

"Why?"

Crossley laughed. "Because they made my car look ugly."

"Why try to kill me?"

"Oh, I had to," said Crossley. "As long as you were out there, the possibility existed that somehow you would find me out. They'd never find Grady, or if they did it would look like a climbing accident. But you hung out there like the sword of Damocles."

"And Ben Tripp? You tried killing him, too, didn't you?"

Crossley's abrupt cackle again, short and nasty. "Indeed, young lady. Indeed. Made rather a botch of it. But I'll do better later tonight."

Kathy's eyes widened and Crossley snapped off another short laugh. "Ah, another love interest,

eh?'' he said. ''My, my, how do you find the
time?''

''Why kill Ben?'' she said in a voice that came
out high and pained.

''Why kill Ben Tripp?'' Crossley made a show
of rubbing his chin and looking toward the ceiling,
as if he was thinking. ''Why kill Ben Tripp? Let's
see, the answer is, um, now what is the answer?
Had it just a minute ago.'' He rubbed his chin some
more. Kathy watched him wild eyed, her back
pushed into the cushion of the sofa. Crossley
snapped his fingers in the air. ''Ah yes! Of course!
Yes. Tidying, my dear, that's all. Don't you see, the
loose ends need to be tidied. A perfect crime, at
first. Grady disappears. Falls from a mountain.
Dead. Perfect. But you''—he jammed the gun toward her and Kathy pushed even farther backward—''but you muck it all up. Bring in this Tripp
fellow and suddenly both of you have suspicions.
Now, your death would drive him into a frenzy.
And my position with a frenzied detective on the
case becomes untenable. So he dies as well. The
mystery ends. You're both dead; the mystery of
Scott Grady's unfortunate demise on a Montana
cliff is buried with you.''

''But they'll find you,'' said Kathy defiantly.

''Probably not,'' said Crossley. ''In fact, what
they'll find is the tragic result of a psychotic's compulsion. Poor Vernon Wells. Pursued you all over
America but couldn't have you. Driven, finally, to
murder...and then suicide.''

Kathy looked at him wide eyed.

A small smile crossed his face. His eyes were
narrow slits. ''Yes, Mr. Wells is dead right now.''

Kathy felt a sob of panic rise through her chest. Crossley held out the pistol. "Killed with this very gun, actually. A suicide, or at least so it will appear. A suicide after he tracked Ben Tripp down and murdered him in cold blood for stealing your affections. A suicide after he dispatched you. He wrote you this poem, or, again, so it will appear. Brought it for you to see before he killed you. You read it. His prints and yours are all over it." Crossley moved closer to her and leveled the gun five inches from her eye. "He shot Tripp, he shot you, and then, sadly, went home and blew his own miserable brains out."

Kathy lunged for the gun and Crossley moved to the side, but she managed to grab it in one hand. Crossley swung his arm violently and wrenched the gun free. He smashed into her with his body and brought the gun down hard on her temple. The nickel-plated steel hit flesh with a soft crunch and Kathy fell back dazed on the floor.

"Down!" he hissed, reeling with the gun to collect his balance. "I'll put you down!"

HUNCHING BELOW the edge of the bedroom window, Tripp made his way silently to the back door. Above the music he could just make out a man's voice. Tripp pushed softly against the door. It opened slowly and light poured out onto the lawn. Tripp ducked back. Listened. The man was still speaking, but he couldn't make out the words. Tripp slipped through the door and flattened himself against the kitchen counter.

KATHY WAS ON HER KNEES on the floor, rubbing blood from her face and trying to pull herself to-

gether. Her head spun and blood in her eyes pushed
the room out of focus. "It won't work," she said,
gasping for breath.

"Oh, but it will," panted the man. "Everything
now pins on poor, sick, befuddled Vernon Wells.
The car crash, the break-in. Everything. And he's
quite dead. Here"—he held out his left hand, the
plastic glove smeared red—"his blood. Quite
dead."

Kathy drew back violently. "You can't do this!"

"Sorry, dear, but you're wrong. *Dead* wrong!"
Crossley leveled the gun at her temple and pulled
back the hammer with an audible click.

TRIPP EDGED ALONG the counter. From the other
room he heard Crossley's voice and then a sound
that seemed to freeze on the air and shatter like
glass against everything Tripp prayed for—the
sound of a trigger being cocked. In a mindless,
thoughtless rage, Tripp launched himself through
the doorway.

Tripp's body hit Crossley like a thunderclap. The
pistol went off. Tripp grabbed Crossley's gun hand
and wrenched it upward. Kathy fell back on the
floor and scuttled like a crab toward the kitchen.
Crossley shoved Tripp backward against the mantel,
pinning him with his weight.

Tripp managed to get both hands on Crossley's
wrist and squeezed the gun hand upward. The pistol
went off against his ear and Tripp was momentarily
deafened. Tripp squirmed sideways and tried grabbing Crossley by the neck. Crossley fought out of
the hold and jammed the gun into Tripp's gut. Tripp

wrenched wildly to the side as Crossley squeezed off a shot. It tore through Tripp's shirt and shattered the lamp. Tripp swung hard and staggered Crossley with a blow to the jaw. Another wild round smashed into the mask on the wall. Tripp ducked, but Crossley brought the handle of the pistol hard across his temple. Blackness flowed across his eyes and Tripp fell to his knees, fighting to hold consciousness. Crossley squeezed off another shot. Almost like a dream, Tripp felt a slug tear into his arm, felt the blow stagger him sideways and headlong into the wall. Tripp's mind dropped into darkness and his body crumpled onto the floor. Crossley let off another round and Tripp's back twitched as the lead seared across flesh.

Crossley staggered backward and fought to control his balance. In the kitchen doorway, Kathy let off a low, guttural scream and ducked toward the hallway. Looking wildly around, Crossley brought his gun up in two hands and staggered after her.

"Dead now!" he gasped. "You're dead now!" He lunged down the hallway toward the bedroom.

Tripp rose through blackness into pain and confusion. His back was on fire and his arm was numb and burning. He staggered to his knees, fighting to keep the vomit down. He put his good hand out against the wall and felt his fist close on a shelf. Summoning strength from somewhere, he lurched to his feet. The room spun and he fell against the bookshelves.

Kathy screamed.

Tripp plunged toward the kitchen. It was empty. Kathy screamed again, and Tripp staggered into the hall. In front of him Crossley's khaki-covered back.

Beyond, the darkened bedroom. Pulling a resolve from some inner depths he had never known, Tripp launched himself in a flying tackle that hit Crossley at the waist. Both men rolled into the bedroom, the pistol skittering across the hardwood floor. Kathy scuttled out of the closet and grabbed the gun. Tripp tried to put a headlock on Crossley, but Crossley squirmed out of it and fell on the floor beside Kathy. She put the gun to Crossley's temple, closed her eyes, and squeezed the trigger. The hammer fell with a hollow click on an empty chamber.

Crossley launched himself out of the room with a scream that seemed primal against the night. Tripp grabbed an arm as he lunged past and both men staggered in a clumsy violent waltz down the hall and back into the living room. Tripp wrenched Crossley's head to the side and they both fell. Crossley found his feet first and snatched a spear from the wall. Tripp clawed to his feet as Crossley came at him, his head down, the spear in front of him, its obsidian tip glinting lethally in the light. Crossley screamed again and Tripp twisted to the side. The spear tip sliced a groove across his belly and Tripp fell back, his good arm flailing through what was left of the framed photos on the mantel. Tripp felt a heavy rock under his hand. He grabbed it. With every ounce of his remaining strength, with Kathy's face floating in his mind, Tripp swung the chunk of ancient bone toward Crossley's face. It caught the professor on the side of the head with such force that waves of pain ripped up Tripp's arm. Tripp twisted to the side and staggered against the wall. Crossley's dying body slowly crumpled to the floor.

Tripp focused his eyes and fought to bring his

breathing under control. His left arm hung useless at his side and burning pains clawed across his stomach and the small of his back. Sirens and flashing lights in the street. From behind him in the bedroom, soft, low, frightened whimpering. Tripp lurched down the hall. Kathy was crouched in the doorway of the closet, blood smeared down across her beautiful face. He crossed the room and knelt. She looked at him desperately. Tripp took her in his arms.

TWENTY-FOUR

A SUNDAY AFTERNOON, and all three horses had crowded into the shade by the barn and were switching at flies with their long tails. Bello had one rear leg crooked back and seemed to be asleep. Across the meadow, the scrub pines shimmered silver green under the hot sun.

"Oh, you stupid…," cried Tripp as he lost his grip on the hose and a stream of icy water shot across his face and down the front of his shirt and pants. He twisted to the side out of the spray and a twinge of pain shot across his lower back. Tripp straightened up and rubbed the spot where Crossley's bullet had grazed his skin. Still sore, but healing. Tripp shook the water off and aimed the nozzle back inside the rusty trough at the stubborn green moss, wiping absently at a few of the slimy strands that had managed to lodge on his cheek.

Behind him the mountain stillness was broken by a car horn.

Tripp turned to watch as a clean new car thumped across the cattle guard and made its way down the short lane, pulling up next to him in a thin cloud of tan dust.

"Howdy, cowboy," said Kathy, emerging from the car. The cast was gone and she was smiling. A small bandage covered her left temple. Tripp thought she looked great.

"Like it?"

"Nice," said Tripp, appreciatively.

"I mean the car." She laughed. "Insurance and a little savings. Has seats with heaters in 'em."

Tripp whistled.

"And I'm thinking about getting a car phone."

Tripp made an ugly face.

"Maybe call you from my car one of these days." Kathy's eyes were bright, teasing.

"Unlikely." Tripp smiled.

Kathy looked toward the barn.

"How's my little Bella?" Kathy made a popping sound with her tongue. "Here, Bella. Come here, Bella."

To Tripp's surprise, the Arab untangled herself from the knot by the barn and made her way lazily across the dusty yard. Kathy held out her hand and Bella nuzzled into it.

"Nice little horse," Kathy cooed, "nice little horse."

"You never cease to amaze me."

"That's a good start," said Kathy. Tripp didn't know if she was talking to him or the horse. "Little barnyard maintenance today, cowboy?"

"Moss is a crop this rancher grows pretty well, thank you." Tripp laughed. "I've given up on the fences."

Kathy reached across and picked a strand of moss from Tripp's face. "Now you're perfect," and she laughed.

Tripp eyed the new car. "Things settling down for you a bit?"

"A bit," said Kathy, scratching Bella's ears, looking off toward the pines. "Police came by again yesterday. Said it'd probably be the last time. Case is pretty well wrapped.''

"Sick little man," observed Tripp.

"Unbelievably."

"Police tell you anything?"

"Some," said Kathy. "The way they figure it, Crossley got wind of Scott's discovery sometime this spring, maybe reading the bills that came in from Harvard. Anyway, he figured it out and tried to move in on it. Scott got scared and gave me a piece of the stuff he'd found. For safekeeping. I thought it was just another rock."

Kathy drew a cigarette out of her slacks and lit it. Her face had clouded. "Then Crossley followed him up to the site and they had a confrontation," she said, "and Crossley pushed Scott off that cliff. Tried to make it look like an accident." She looked back at her new car. "They found Scott's motorbike down in the stream at the mouth of the canyon."

Tripp nodded and remained silent. He'd already heard most of it through Bowen's friends.

"Guess it spooked Crossley when I called him. Broke into my place, broke into Scott's.looking for evidence that would tie him to the murder. Erased Scott's research from the computer. Found the fossil at my place. Then, the first chance he got, he came after me. Police checked. He never showed up for the Great Falls meeting. Came after me—and then came after you." She said it simply and Tripp realized the horror, at least, was past. The pain, he knew, would linger.

"They ever find any more of Scott's climbing notes?" asked Tripp, his voice gentle.

"Nothing in the office or the apartment," said

Kathy. "And nothing in Crossley's effects. Police went through Crossley's stuff right before the funeral. Nothing." She picked at the moss in the trough.

"Didn't find Scott's dissertation then, either?"

"No sign of it," said Kathy. "John Hunt and Corry are going to take over the site and do the study all over. Plan to publish it under Scott's name." Her eyes were firmly on the tree line. "Detective handling the case thinks Crossley was holding up Corry's dissertation because he thought it might give away the secret. Sick man."

"So Corry's sticking around?"

"Looks that way."

The two were quiet for a time, watching the horses, listening to the mountains.

"What about the Js?" said Kathy. "Anybody ever figure that out?"

"Don't think anybody knows what the Js actually stood for," said Tripp. "A code. Guess nobody's ever gonna break it."

Belli had walked up and was trying to insert himself between Kathy and the little Arab.

"Donner?" said Kathy.

"Donner," said Tripp. "Strange man. I guess he's still around. I haven't heard."

"Ever find out why he lied about the Idaho trip?" Kathy asked.

"Never asked."

"How's Nathan?"

"Healing," said Tripp. "Couple of pretty good whacks to the head. He'll have a scar to remember this by. But that's all."

Kathy's eyes grew tender. "And how's Ben Tripp?"

Tripp self-consciously rubbed the bullet scar on his arm. "Healing nicely, thank you." He smiled. "What now for you?"

"Get on with life," said Kathy, turning her head to hide the tears welling in her eyes. She scratched furiously at Bella's mane. "Vernon Wells' parents came out from Boston to take the body home. They came by and we talked for a time. I gave them the poems." A teardrop coursed down her cheek. "I thought about moving, getting out of here. But I like it here, despite all this. Figure I'll stay. Maybe try to put down some roots." She smiled shyly.

"Here," said Tripp, handing Kathy the hose. "Spray it around in there for a minute. I'll be right back."

Some faint metallic clanks and a thud and a curse echoed out of the shop. At length, Tripp came out carrying a couple of shovels and a bucket and trying to lick at his thumb.

"What are you doing?" Kathy asked, forgetting the tears.

"Banged my hand."

"No, I mean the stuff."

"Know this little spot up in the mountains," said Tripp. "We're gonna go dig some gold."

Was it justice...vengeance...or both!

LYNN ERICKSON

THE RIPPLE EFFECT

The celebrity murder trial of Robbie Childress resulted in an acquittal that shocked the nation and devastated the family of the victim, Robbie's wife. Then Robbie is shot to death and Lawrence Bergen, his former father-in-law, stands accused.

Tess Bergen possesses a devastating secret that can make or break the case for her father's defense—and it's private investigator Dan Hadley's job to find it. As the courtroom drama unfolds, Tess and Dan dare to trust and to love as the ripple effect reaches a shattering conclusion as real as today's headlines.

"Lynn Erickson joins the ranks of Sandra Brown and Nora Roberts." —*The Paperback Forum*

On sale mid-March 1999 wherever paperbacks are sold!

MIRA

MURDER AT THE MOVIES

CHARLENE WEIR
GEORGE BAXT
MAXINE O'CALLAGHAN

MURDER TAKE TWO
by Charlene Weir

Hollywood comes to Hampstead, Kansas, with the filming of a
new picture starring sexy actress Laura Edwards. But murder
steals the scene when a stunt double is impaled on a pitchfork.

THE HUMPHREY BOGART MURDER CASE
by George Baxt

Hollywood in its heyday is brought to life in this witty caper
featuring a surprise sleuth—Humphrey Bogart. While filming
The Maltese Falcon, he searches for a real-life treasure, dodging
a killer on a murder trail through Hollywood.

SOMEWHERE SOUTH OF MELROSE
by Maxine O'Callaghan

P.I. Delilah West is hired to search for an old high school
classmate. The path takes her through the underbelly of broken
dreams and into the caprices of fate, where secrets are born and
sometimes kept....

Available March 1999 at your favorite retail outlet.

MIND GAMES

C.J. KOEHLER

A RAY KOEPP MYSTERY

Searching for a killer's motivation requires logic and insight into human nature, skills at which former priest Ray Koepp excels.

The victim is Isaac Steiner, a prominent man in academic circles and founder of Friar's Close, a housing community conceived as a refuge from urban violence.

As Koepp begins to investigate, he confronts the myriad sides of human nature, and discovers life at Friar's Close is far from idyllic.

Available May 1999 at your favorite retail outlet.